"I don't like you one bit tonight, Reverend. Get your hands off me," Dee demanded, furious at Matt and God and the world.

"What's wrong?" He pulled her close, his hands relaying an angry sensuality, a contrasting tenderness that was too enticing for her to reject with conviction.

"Maybe you didn't hear me. I said—"

"Hush your mouth. Hush it before I do it for you." He took her hand and raised it to his mouth and nibbled on the heel of her palm. Eager first, then leisurely. Her fury was stunned into silence. He handled her as if she were a wildcat he was soothing into submission. Indeed, he coaxed a purr.

"Stop—stop it, Matt."

"I don't want to stop. And judging by the way you're moving against me, stopping's the last thing you want from me." His fingertips traced a slow, burning path down her spine, and her skin grew hot everywhere he touched.

"You shouldn't be doing this." Her voice was more a gasp, a languorous sigh, than a protest.

"Why not? Because I'm a minister who's supposed to be more than human?"

She didn't know what they were talking about anymore. All she knew was that both his hands were on her, moving over the thin silk, stroking her and making it impossible to think. . . .

WHAT ARE *LOVESWEPT* ROMANCES?

They are stories of true romance and touching emotion. We believe those two very important ingredients are constants in our highly sensual and very believable stories in the *LOVESWEPT* line. Our goal is to give you, the reader, stories of consistently high quality that may sometimes make you laugh, sometimes make you cry, but are always fresh and creative and contain many delightful surprises within their pages.

Most romance fans read an enormous number of books. Those they truly love, they keep. Others may be traded with friends and soon forgotten. We hope that each *LOVESWEPT* romance will be a treasure—a "keeper." We will always try to publish

LOVE STORIES YOU'LL NEVER FORGET
BY AUTHORS YOU'LL ALWAYS REMEMBER

The Editors

Loveswept® 569

Olivia Rupprecht
Saints and Sinners

BANTAM BOOKS
NEW YORK · TORONTO · LONDON · SYDNEY · AUCKLAND

SAINTS AND SINNERS

A Bantam Book / September 1992

*If you would be interested in receiving protective vinyl
covers for your Loveswept books, please write to this address
for information:*

*Loveswept
Bantam Books
P.O. Box 985
Hicksville, NY 11802*

ISBN 0-553-44122-1

Published simultaneously in the United States and Canada

Saints and Sinners

One

The final strains of organ music blended with the heavy beat of rock and roll. Outside the nonde-nominational Peace Church's open doors, Rev. Matthew Peters shook the last hand in line. He smiled into Maude's weathered face before she darted a glance across the street and harrumphed at Billy Joel's preference of laughing with sinners over crying with saints.

"The choir did a fine job this morning, Maude," he said kindly. Matt wondered what old Maude would think about preachers breaking command-ments. He had just lied. "If everyone sang with as much enthusiasm as you do, we'd be heard clear across Iowa."

"'Make a joyful noise unto the Lord,' the Good Book says, and I surely do my best, Reverend Matthew."

If that was her best, he'd hate to hear her worst. It was noise all right, and he could only hope the congregation took his bowed head as prayerful. His sides still hurt from holding in a belly laugh while Maude warbled the postlude.

"Our best is all any of us can do, Maude. We all stumble." He cocked his ear to pick up the last of the rock lyrics which coincided with the bang of a screen door. "Saints and sinners alike." Matthew chuckled.

"You never sit in judgment, Reverend. Maybe that's why you make us feel like you're one of us, not one of those archangels that're flying so high they can't pass for mortal."

"Believe me, I'm as mortal as the next ma—" The word was cut short by what he saw across the street. "Man," he finished, clearing his throat.

The pleasure he felt in watching the woman put down a box on the front porch, then stretch, causing her halter to rise, left no doubt of his being a man. Even a preacher could appreciate God's craftsmanship in the form of long legs in short cutoffs, a pretty face, and judging from the swish of her ponytail, a generous length of hair the color of sunshine.

With difficulty he forced his attention back to Maude. She'd followed his gaze and pursed her lips.

"That woman ought to be arrested for indecent exposure, prancing around in next to nothing."

"It's warm outside." Warm? It seemed closer to a scorcher as he glanced at the woman once more and watched as she arched her neck and pressed a can against it. The can moved lower, lower, until she rolled it over her cleavage, apparently unaware she was being observed, much less discussed. Matthew's white cotton clergy robes began to feel more like a wool blanket on a sticky summer night.

"Why don't you go over and welcome her to the community, Maude? Maybe invite her to next Sunday's pot luck lunch? You are head of the visitation committee."

"Sorry, Reverend. I have a family reunion and eggs waiting to be . . . deviled." Her aged lips twitched into a grin.

Matthew laughed good-naturedly while he suppressed an inner sigh. A quick surge of empathy came fast on the heels of the enjoyment he'd taken in the woman's feminine curves. He'd heard the rumors, of course. News travels fast in rural small towns like Hayes, Iowa. Especially when it involves an attractive single woman who was reportedly divorced not once, but twice. With her last name being different from that of her two children, what else could it be? And the children were far too old for her not to have had them when she was little more than a child herself.

He wondered if she had any idea the local gossip mill had dubbed her an undesirable before she'd unloaded the first box.

After bidding Maude a good week and a "God be with you," Matt paused at the church doors. He could walk a couple of blocks to his empty parsonage and heat up some leftovers. Or accept one of the standing invitations to Sunday dinner. Or go to the local restaurant and join any number of people who would unceasingly smile, delineate their woes, apologize for not making it to church, or clean up their conversation as if he were too removed from everyday life to hear a curse word without flinching.

Or he could do the right thing.

Shutting the doors but leaving them unlocked, Matthew proceeded across the street, his robes fluttering against his legs with the dry wisp of a mid-September breeze.

"'Afternoon, neighbor," he called when she turned for the front door. A second's awareness passed between them, and he identified the look she gave him. It said, I'll pretend I didn't notice you were coming over if you'll pretend I didn't see you, and please spare me a church visit, preacher man. He waved anyway and said, "Welcome to Hayes!"

"Er . . . thanks." *Damn.* Just what she needed. *More* nosy questions and an invitation to church from the pulpit pounder himself.

Delilah eyed him warily while he took the few steps up to the porch. She'd seen how he walked across the street—with purpose, a sort of energetic stride. And now he was smiling. A big, open, sincere smile that wasn't quite right, because it was kind of sexy, too, and everyone knew ministers were not sexy. They were genitalless. Like parents.

"Matthew Peters." He extended his hand.

"Delilah Sampson." She hesitated, then grasped his hand. Warm. Strong. Large. Pleasant. But most of all . . . warm.

"Let's see, you go by Dee, right?"

"How did you know?" She took her hand back quickly, not liking the familiarity small towns bred.

"Your landlord told me. Mrs. Davis is a church member. Nice lady."

"Hmmm. Yes." Dee had to agree. By the time she'd found the neat-as-a-pin cottage two days before, she was desperate. In Las Vegas you plunked down a deposit and moved in. In Hayes strangers seemed to be suspect, judging from all the personal questions that she was asked. Here the fitness of a renter was based on reputation rather than cash. Not that that was something a minister could relate to, what with being untouched by the world's uglier side.

"Small towns can take some getting used to. Especially after living in a big city."

"I guess she told you that too." He probably knew her underwear size to boot.

"Nope. I just picked up certain vibes from you."

Vibes? Though dated, the word still seemed too hip for a man of the cloth to toss out. Just as the way he was hitching up his robe, propping a booted foot on the box she'd hid her beer behind, and flashing her that too-sexy smile again was not what she thought of as standard minister behavior.

"What kind of vibes?" she asked cautiously.

"Oh . . . like you wish I'd get the Hades out of here and leave you alone."

What was he, a mind reader? Or were her nerves so shot from ordeals and more ordeals that she behaved as snippily and on guard as she felt? *That wasn't smart*, not to mention a lack of good manners.

"I'm terribly sorry. I didn't mean to be rude. Especially to a—"

"Hey, no sweat. Rough time getting settled?"

"*Rough. Very rough.*" Why was she telling him this? Letting anyone get too personal, even a minister, was out of the question. Though the way he was nodding his head and making her feel he understood and sympathized was about the kindest welcome she'd had in a very long time. Dee stepped back, away from the lure of his silent offering. "What I mean is, I like my privacy and that's a scarce commodity here."

"You're right. Sometimes I miss having a bit of anonymity myself."

"You?"

"Even ministers like their privacy. Especially ones like me, who come from a big city. I've only been here six months, and people . . . well, they're friendly and they've been very accepting, of course. But for some reason folks tend to put ministers in a sanctified slot, on a pedestal where they don't necessarily belong or want to be." He quirked a dark brow and scratched his head. "Beats me why they do it. Seems to be an occupational hazard."

Dee laughed. She laughed for the first time in what seemed ages. This reverend wasn't like any reverend she'd ever known. His dark hair was ruffled, a little long and just as sexy as his smile. His eyes were hazel and seemed a lot older than the rest of his face, which appeared thirtysomething. She liked his eyes best of all, she decided. They were so vibrant, they sort of . . . twinkled.

"So, Rev., why did you leave the big city to come here?"

The twinkle vanished. "Same reason a lot of people move to small towns. There's a sense of community and trust. I can leave the church doors unlocked, without worrying about vandalism, for anyone who might have a need to be there. Peace."

Peace was not what she saw in his eyes. There was something in him that she picked up on because it was so strongly in her own bones. A need not to be alone, to touch a kindred spirit, at the same time wanting to shut everyone and everything away. It had to be a trick of lighting, she decided. A man of God couldn't possibly share those feelings.

And he most certainly wouldn't be staring at her with interest. Masculine interest.

Without meaning to, she glanced at his left hand. No ring. Just a large, well-shaped hand dusted lightly with hair. When she looked up she realized the twinkle was back. He'd caught her looking! And judging from the flash of even white teeth that showed in his grin, the regard was mutual.

"Dee!" Delilah spun around in time to see thirteen-year-old Loren burst through the door, screaming at the top of her lungs. "Jason's got my favorite tape and he won't give it back!"

"Who cares?" yelled back Jason, who was ten.

"Dork. Dweeb."

"Kids, *please!*" Delilah glared at them both. "We have company," she said between clenched teeth. "This is Rev. Peters. What do you say?"

When Loren continued to sulk and said nothing, Jason had the good manners to shuffle his feet in embarrassment.

"How do you do, Rev. Peters," he said politely.

"Call me Rev. Matthew, Jason. Made any new friends yet?"

"No, sir. Dee said we have to be patient."

"They start school tomorrow," Dee explained.

"We'll be the new faces when everyone else knows each other." Loren pouted. "Yuck. I hate school already."

"But you'll be a pretty new face." Delilah gave her a hug. "And Jason's always the best on any team. You'll both do fine."

"Sure you will." Matthew agreed as if he had divine assurance it was true. "If the two of you want to come to a pizza party the youth group's having on Wednesday, you're welcome to join us. Good way to make some new friends, and the pizza's not bad either."

"Can we?" Jason said with excitement. "Dee, please?"

Dee looked at Matthew's friendly smile to Jason's expectant face. As much as she wanted to keep a low profile and not get involved, it was proving impossible. And the kids needed friendship and acceptance. Desperately.

"You're invited too, Dee. Chances are the other kids might take you as an older sis—" Matthew coughed. "I'm sure most women wish they looked as young for their age as you do."

Delilah pursed her lips. Maybe she should test the waters, find out how Matthew Peters juggled honesty with tact, occupational hazards being what they were. Besides, she wanted to know what the locals did think of her.

"And just how old do you take me for?" *C'mon, Mr. Minister, thou shan't lie, even if you'd like nothing better right about now.*

"Ah . . . let's see. Somewhere in your late twenties, early thirties perhaps? I never was very good at judging age."

"How very diplomatic. Sure you're not in politics instead of the ministry?"

"Sometimes I think they're related fields." Matthew laughed easily, inducing Delilah to join him. She felt she should be ashamed of herself for baiting him, but found his candid humor too refreshing to regret her behavior. This guy was okay. Better than okay. He was devilishly attractive and personable, even if he was a minister. And it would be so good to make a friend. . . .

She squelched the thought as well as her laughter. "The truth is, I'm twenty-seven. Loren's thirteen and Jason's ten," she said with a pointed gaze.

Matthew met her challenging stare. The way he shrugged as if to say, So? made her feel that he was far more comfortable and unconcerned with her status than she.

"Can I have a look at that tape, Jason?" With admirable grace he diffused the momentary tenseness. "Hammer. Rap. I've got some rap tunes at the church."

"That's totally awesome," Jason exclaimed.

"We're hip." Snapping his fingers, he chanted in a raspy voice.

"Get real, get God. Sin's a drag and can't you see? Main Man on Sweet Char-i-ot. Yo! Yo, He's watchin' over me. Be cosmic. Be cool. Brother, get this Golden Rule. Love that neighbor, love yo' self. S'cool. S'cool."

"Wow." Jason took the word out of Dee's mouth when Matt finished with a rapid foot shuffle. Loren pinched her lips together, refusing to smile or acknowledge the minister could give Vanilla Ice a run for his rap money.

"We'll play some others at the pizza party, so

you can check them out. Here's your tape back, Loren."

She stared at his outstretched hand. Dee flushed. Just as she was about to reach for the tape herself, Loren took it.

"Thanks," she muttered, then whirled to go back inside. The screen door banged behind her. Dee shut her eyes and prayed for strength.

A rock to crawl under would be nice too.

"Jason, could you please finish unpacking your things?"

"Aw, Dee, do I have to?"

"Young man," she said in a warning tone.

"Got a football stashed with your stuff?"

"You bet I do, Rev. Matthew."

"If it's okay with your mom, we can pass it later, after all your things are put away. You know, nice and neat, the way moms like it."

"All right!"

"But one condition. Big guys like you and me, we don't get off on messing with girl stuff. Even tapes. Right?"

"Right. Yo!" Jason was gone in a flash.

Matthew chuckled. "Piece of cake." Then he winked.

He winked? At her? As if they were co-conspirators. And since when did ministers wink at women they just met and flash too-sexy smiles? This was not in the game plan. Not his easy insinuation into their family and most definitely not this unexpected attraction she was experiencing. His hands. His eyes. His lips. She couldn't reconcile his appearance or personality with his profession.

She was suspicious. Then again, she had learned to be suspicious of all men, more so than even poor Loren.

"I'm sure you must be busy, Rev. Peters. Too busy to—"

"Matt."

"I beg your pardon?"

"Please, call me Matt. First name minus the title."

"I was raised in a conservative church. Calling a minister by his first name seems a little inappropriate."

"No more than kids calling a mother by her first name." He said it without censure, just the statement of a fact she couldn't argue. "And I'm not too busy today to pass a football. You know us ministers, loafing on the job once the Sunday sermon's over. Besides, I'd enjoy it. Don't you think Jason would too?"

For such a clean-cut kind of guy, he sure knew how to play dirty. She hesitated, then gave a curt nod.

"About Loren. I apologize for her behavior. It was inexcusable."

"No problem. She's at a tough age, but she'll outgrow it."

"Not soon enough to suit me. If I survive Loren, it'll be a miracle."

"You'll survive."

"How can you be so sure?"

"Because I believe in miracles."

Something warm and fuzzy and delicious seemed to spark in his eyes. Before she could deflect it, it reached down inside her and filled up an empty place that life had hollowed out. She had a sudden urge to touch him, to discover if the feel of him was half as moving or good as the almost tactile sensation his gaze created.

With difficulty Dee broke the visual bond and hoisted a large fern from the box on the porch.

"Speaking of miracles," she said brightly, "I don't think they extend to boxes unpacking themselves. Thanks for coming by, Rev—Matt. I'm sure Jason will look forward to seeing you later."

Reaching up to hang the fern on a hook, she missed by several inches.

When she stood on tiptoe and strained higher, Matt edged closer, his voice oddly tight. "I'll get that."

Their hands brushed. White cotton met naked thigh.

She felt a distinct ripple, a tingle, where they touched. Looking up at him, Delilah felt the earlier warmth inside spread. Just as sweet. Just as welcome. But intense.

Chemical. Earthy. And something more.

This time it was he who broke their locked gazes. Matt hung the fern, then quickly stepped away. As he pivoted, his foot hit the box.

Delilah watched, appalled, when the box angled into her hidden can. It tipped, seemingly in slow motion. Yellow fizz gurgled onto the hem of his robe.

"Oh, God," she groaned. Dee dropped to her knees and reached into the box for a rag. "Oh, God, I'm sorry."

"The name's Matt, Dee. Matt."

"I'm sorry, Matt. I'm—"

"Hey, it's no big deal."

She swiped the rag over the white cloth, then groaned some more when she saw that she'd managed only to grind plant soil into the soaked cotton. Wiping and rubbing only made it worse.

"This is so embarrassing, so—"

"Dee." He patted her shoulder. "It'll wash off. Really."

His voice was as reassuring as his touch. It was also disconcerting. Her head bent, she studied the mess she'd made of his robe. Dee saw the two of them as an outsider would, her kneeling at his feet like some penitent, pleading, "Forgive me, Father, for I have sinned," and his gesture of "You are forgiven. Now rise, my child, and sin no more."

Yet his light, comforting touch conveyed no hint of benevolence. In fact, it was downright exciting, and if thinking about a minister that way was sinful, then she was a sinner, no question. An unrepentant one at that.

Delilah looked up, a final apology on her lips. The words froze and so did she. Matthew's gaze was on her cleavage, which was an eyeful, she belatedly realized. This wasn't her usual dress, but she'd been so hot, so . . . He shut his eyes, appearing to be caught in some internal struggle.

Did ministers have the capacity to lust? Not that she considered herself a woman who often commanded that kind of reaction from men. And this wasn't exactly a man. He was a minister, for heaven's sake.

When Matthew opened his eyes, they were carefully trained on her face. He managed a thin smile before he grasped her upper arms and helped her to her feet.

"I'll be glad to wash that, Matt."

"No need. But if you're determined to absolve yourself, you can offer me a drink. It's, ah, warmer than usual today." He let go of her arms as if they were the source of the heat.

"I have some soft drinks. Or I can make lemonade."

"I don't know, Dee, that's some pretty stiff brew you're talking there." He grinned and that pulse-pounding, heart-dropping twinkle of his nearly knocked her again to her knees. "If you've got an extra, I'd really prefer a beer."

Two

"A beer?"

"Sure. You know, a brew, a barley pop, lite or regular. I'm not picky."

"But—but what would your church think?"

Matthew's smile faded. He knew too well that some people thought they were God and everyone had to conform to their standards. It's done and over with, he told himself. Let it go.

Letting go wasn't easy.

"About that beer," he said after a moment. "My church won't mind if you don't. But if that offends your principles, I'll gladly take the soda or lemonade."

"No. No, I'm not offended. Just . . ." She worried her bottom lip. Lips he thought exquisitely crafted, bowed at the top and full beneath. A beauty mark rode low on her right cheek, and it disappeared into a dimple when she smiled. She smiled now. "I was just taken aback. Well, shocked actually. My church wasn't that progressive."

"Everyone's entitled to his or her own opinions and choice of faith." He saw her nod of agreement, then stooped to pick up the can.

He remembered the sight of Dee's bent head

gleaming golden in the sunlight, her almost comical frenzy to dry his robe. He remembered the distinct sensation of pleasure when his palm touched her shoulder, the warmth of her skin beneath the thin fabric of her halter top. And there was no forgetting the beauty of those partially uncovered breasts he'd struggled to ignore, and, failing that, admired. Only he'd more than admired them; his reaction had been that of a man wishing for more than a look.

As he straightened, his face nearly brushed her bare legs. Lovely legs that were slender at the ankles and curved delicately upward. When he reached her thighs, Matthew jerked his attention away. *Temptation.* It had been absent for quite some time.

Another test, Lord? I'm still recovering from the last one, even if it wasn't half as intriguing as this. Think You could grant me some immunity this go-round?

Matthew handed Delilah the can. Their fingers brushed. *No immunity today, huh? Well, didn't hurt to ask.* She lowered her gaze and smiled demurely before leading them into the house. The provocative sway of her hips as she headed for the kitchen caused Matt to whistle silently. Definitely no immunity today.

"Nice place you've got here," he noted when she returned.

"Once we're settled, I think it'll be cozy. Maybe a little too cozy."

"How's that?"

"The kids' bedrooms are upstairs." She looked above her, less to indicate the location than to take her eyes off one heck of a hunk, who was disrobing. "I can hear every squeak of their beds and every step when they walk. Since they'd rather run than walk, it usually sounds like a cattle call overhead. If there was more than one bedroom down here, we could switch floors, but at least I get some peace and quiet once they're asleep and I'm alone and . . ."

His gaze moved in tandem with hers to her open bedroom door and the unmade bed. The slight distance between them seemed to vanish as an intimate pull took hold.

Matthew smiled, a slow smile that somehow strengthened the disconcerting bond, then laid his folded robe and tie on the couch that had come with the furnished cottage. Two pangs struck her without warning or mercy.

One was for having to leave her own possessions behind, especially the baby grand piano she wanted to weep for losing. The other pang, which was more like a jolt, was upon seeing Matt in a shirt with rolled-up sleeves and a pair of pressed denim jeans. His build was athletic but lean, and she imagined his body was rock solid.

"Your beer, Reverend." She emphasized his title, hoping to douse her delicious awareness of this man.

"Why do I get the feeling that I'm destroying my exalted image? Let's see if I can recoup." He tapped his can to hers. "May you make many happy memories in your new home and find peace wherever you live."

"Amen to that." Talk about miracles, she thought grimly, and took a few swallows. Matthew matched her gulp for gulp, then put down his can. She lingered over a few more sips, then reached for his robe. "Make yourself comfortable while I wash this." She was gone before he could protest.

Glad for the excuse to put some space between them, Dee indulged her curiosity and inspected the large garment.

A distinctly masculine scent rose up from the cloth, and, closing her eyes, she inhaled deeply. How long had it been since she'd nuzzled a man's neck? Tasted the flavor of skin, felt the keen rub of whiskers against her face, or heard the low groan of an intimate command?

Dee jerked her nose out of the robe and stared at it. What was she, depraved? Maybe she hadn't gone to church in years or indulged in intimate fondling, but religious garb and flights of sensual fantasy just didn't mix.

She turned on the faucet and ran cold water over the stain, soaping and scrubbing at a furious speed, as if she could cleanse her forbidden thoughts as well. A warm breeze blew in from the open window over the sink. She flicked water over her flushed cheeks, grateful for the cooling drops.

Just as she finished, she spotted her neighbor, Mrs. Henderson, bent over a flower bed. "Mrs. Busybody," as Dee had dubbed her, was the type who dug for dirt on others and spread it around in the name of community interest.

Mrs. Henderson was not going to be pleased when she learned her new neighbor would soon be competing for piano students.

"I unpacked my clothes, Dee. I'm going for a walk."

"Okay, Loren, but be back before—" She stopped when she glanced over her shoulder and saw the tight tank top and short shorts Loren was wearing. "And just where do you think you're going dressed like *that*?"

"Don't worry, I won't get in a car with any strangers and a two-year-old couldn't get lost in this stupid hellhole if he tried."

"Watch your mouth, young lady." When Loren rolled her eyes and brushed past, Dee dropped the robe and stepped in front of her. Loren's eyes, even with hers, sparked defiantly. "You're not leaving this house until you change your clothes."

"I think they're cool. Besides, I bought this with *my* money, so you can't take it away."

"When and where did you get it? You haven't—"

"No, I haven't snuck off anywhere." Loren sighed dramatically. "Like I could the way we have to get your permission to even breathe. I picked it out at that store in whatever state we were in last week while you were busy buying dishes and sheets."

"The kind of attention you're asking for with those clothes isn't the type you want," Dee said firmly.

"You mean not the type *you* want. Except maybe with that dumb minister you were slobbering over. Just because my father's a jerk—"

"Don't talk about him now." Dee glanced uneasily at the open kitchen door.

Taking advantage of her distraction, Loren stepped around her and rushed out the back door.

"God help me." Picking up the robe, Dee buried her face in it. She pressed her mouth into the fabric to keep from screaming, hugged it close to absorb any remnants of strength or wisdom its wearer might have left within the folds.

What am I going to do? she silently cried. *How am I ever going to get through this? I need help. A miracle. I need—*

"Dee, hope you don't mind, but I helped Jason finish up. He's out front waiting to— Dee? Is something wrong?"

She quickly thrust the material under the spigot. Mascara stained the collar, she realized with dismay, and began to scrub in earnest.

"No, of course not. Everything's fine." The pitch of her voice was too high, too animated. "Thanks for helping Jason get settled."

Throat tight with the effort of control, she willed Matt to go away. Far, far away. At least until she got a grip on herself and washed the mascara out.

"Is it Loren?"

The fine hair on her nape rose as if static, not warm breath, fanned it. He stood behind her, at a respectful distance, but close enough that she felt laps of energy transmitted from his body. Or soul. Or wherever ministers got that certain something that whispered of calm assurance. If she turned and took a single step, she could rest against his chest and find the comfort she needed.

If she turned, he'd see tear tracks on her cheeks, a silent admission of vulnerability she couldn't share.

"It's nothing," she said dismissively. "I'll bring you and Jason a sandwich after I finish with this."

"If you rub any harder at that mascara, there won't be any material left to clean. C'mon, you can talk to me if you need someone to listen. I'm real good at it. At least, if practice makes perfect."

Dee closed her eyes, allowing his deep voice to seep into her and trickle soothingly into the empty places.

"Thanks, Matt. But it's my problem." One of them anyway. A minor one in comparison to the rest. When he didn't move or speak, she decided he was used to waiting people out, being nice and understanding until they broke.

Breaking was a luxury she couldn't afford.

"Look," she said abruptly, "I'm sure you're very good at what you do, listening and consoling and saving lost souls. But I'm not shopping for any of that, so you might as well save your services for someone who wants them. I don't, okay?"

Matthew studied the rigid line of her body, from her neck, down her spine to her slightly spread legs. Everything about her declared resistance. While the counselor in him said to offer a final word of empathy, then back off, his masculine instincts sent a conflicting message.

He leaned into the provocative murmur of those

instincts. It lured him to move closer to her, to envision her tapered ruby nails raking seductively down his back, over his chest, then delving low to stir his loins.

Matt shoved his hands into his suddenly too tight pockets before he acted on the compulsion to touch her. He'd encountered temptation before, but nothing like this. And never, *never* would he disregard another's needs to selfishly see to his own. Such was not his purpose in this life.

And yet wouldn't her neck taste sweet and earthy? Wasn't the small of her back made for a man's tongue, the inside of her knees a place for wet kisses?

"I'm in no position to try saving your soul, Dee," he said gruffly. "Not when my own's in need of repair." That tidbit of confession brought her head up fast. The full sight of her face only increased his awareness that something strange yet wonderful was happening to him.

Propping a hip beside the sink, Matt nodded to temptation—a safe, acceptable nod—and placed a palm over her wet hands.

"Just for the record," he added, "I'm not the one who does the saving. That's a private matter between an individual and his Maker. That said, let's see about putting this robe to the best use it's had all day."

The crook of his finger fit neatly beneath the soft underside of her chin. The damp fabric glided smoothly over the high planes of her cheekbones as he wiped away the smudged makeup.

Openly amazed, she stared at him with the clearest blue eyes he'd ever seen. Tears had a way of cleansing, but even before he'd caught her crying he'd noticed her eyes were luminous, like a lake so clear you could toss in a rock and watch it sink beneath the ripples.

"See? I told you I was good at this kind of stuff.

Gets me a lot of invites to dinner. Good thing, since I can't cook worth a damn. Oops, can't say that word, can I? Strike damn, insert darn."

She laughed. Her eyes danced when she laughed, even when she was so obviously weary with worry. He continued wiping her face though the last traces of mascara were gone.

"Is that a hint that I owe you dinner, Reverend?"

"Far be it from me to invite myself, since I come complete with good manners. On top of being generous and tolerant and amusing and—"

"Don't forget humble."

"Especially humble. And *lonely*." He sighed. Being lonely was too familiar to him, and there were many times when he'd keenly felt the burden of going through life alone. But those things seemed of no substance at the moment, not when he was relishing the feel of Dee's skin beneath his finger.

"Just think, Dee, while you're sitting at the table with Jason and Loren, I'll be all by myself at home, eating Maude's leftover deviled eggs. If I'm lucky, maybe she'll throw in a piece of pie."

"You poor man." Dee's laughter soothed him, a balm of humor and connection he needed more than any soul on earth could possibly know. "Please. Stay for dinner."

"Ah, the old guilt trip. Works every time."

"You'll probably regret it, Matt."

"Not half as much as Loren." When Dee agreed with a snicker, he joined her and felt the connection grow stronger. "Think she'll close her eyes when I say grace?"

"Not if she thinks you're peeking to find out."

"Then maybe we should keep ours open. Give her some incentive to shut hers out of defiance."

Her carefree mood suddenly disappeared, and the chuckle in her voice was gone when she said, "I'm very worried about her, Matt."

"I know you are." He searched her eyes and

nodded sympathetically while his fingers pulsed at the tips, begging for a more personal acquaintance with her skin.

"I won't ask what the situation is," he said quietly. "Not unless it's something you need, or want, to share. But I've seen that expression you're wearing too many times. It's one parents have when they feel they're dealing with a problem bigger than themselves. Just try to remember that you're not alone with the difficulty you're facing."

"I know I'm not the only one with a problem child."

"That's not what I meant." He dabbed at the moisture in the corner of her eye. "You have strength inside you. Trust it. Have faith."

"I am strong," she said slowly. "At least I try to be. But as for faith . . ." An edge of bitterness crept into her soft, alluring features.

"Where is your faith, Dee?"

"I lost it years ago. In my fellow man anyway."

"In life?"

"Sometimes I think so."

"But what about faith in yourself?"

"That's something I'm struggling with."

"Then join the club. Everyone does from time to time."

Her narrowed gaze challenged his claim. "Maybe most people, but you don't qualify, do you?"

"That's news to me. We're talking about being human, and I do qualify, the same as you or anyone else." Times like this he wished he didn't. He wished he were God. Then he'd have the power to make what was bad go away and assure Dee that everything would be all right. But life just wasn't that neat. He wasn't God and the world held no guarantees.

Especially for a wayward minister who had been expelled from his former church for being a heretic.

"You're good at your job, Matthew, you know that?"

"I'm afraid not everyone would agree, but I'm glad you believe so. Maybe you'll visit next Sunday and tell everyone what a great sermon I preach."

"Trying to fill an empty pew?" She smiled slightly and he knew a powerful want to help her shine in the face of adversity.

"The front rows tend to be the most available. Can you imagine what that does to my ego when everyone moves as far back from me as they can get? You'd think I didn't shower or gargle before ringing the bells."

"Maybe you need an incentive. Something like bonus points at the Pearly Gates."

"How about a pot luck lunch next week? All you can eat and there's no charge."

"If I didn't know better, I'd take that as a bribe."

"And a bribe it is. Just goes to prove how devious we ministers can get to beat the competition when a prospective member moves to town."

"And are you . . . devious, Reverend?" She touched his hand and grinned, a feminine curve of the lips that was too genuine and naturally sensual to pass for coy.

Matthew couldn't answer. There was a tightness in his chest that made even breathing difficult. Too many questions were barreling through his brain; too many sensations were erupting from her light, impulsive touch.

He'd never experienced anything like this before, and his experience was not shallow. How incredibly . . . incredible. It felt almost . . . divine? Yes, divine, and preordained.

"Umm . . . Matthew?" Her voice was soft. "If you wipe my face one more time, I'll be so clean that I'll squeak louder than the kids' floors."

He paused in mid-stroke. He wanted to kiss her. Thoroughly. Full on the lips. A lingering exploration that gave no pretense to chastity or virtuous restraint.

He dropped the cloth and slowly traced her parted lips with his fingertip, signaling his intent. Her eyes dilated until they were almost black. Matt savored the anticipation of their mouths melding.

"Rev. Matthew! Rev. Matthew, c'mon! Let's burn some pigskin." Jason's voice and the sound of his footsteps running across the living room floor shattered the silence.

"I think you're being paged." Dee sounded relieved, yet her expression matched his own disappointment.

"For once I wish I didn't have call waiting." The mood had been broken, but not the want. He ran a fingertip over her bottom lip, then pushed away from the sink and turned as Jason appeared in the doorway. "I've got a pack of gum that says you can't beat me outside," he said to the boy.

"Gum? You're on, Rev. Matthew." Jason spun around and raced away.

With a smile, Matthew faced Dee. "Bought us five more minutes."

"Pot luck lunches and gum. Really, Reverend, this habit you have of bribing . . ." Her laugh was shaky. So were her hands when he pressed them between his. "What's next? A six-pack of soda or—my goodness, don't tell me you might graduate to candy bars."

He didn't want to engage in more easy banter. Indeed, he viewed his conduct with Dee as very serious business.

"We need to talk about what happened before Jason interrupted."

"There's nothing to discuss." She jerked her hands from his. "Because nothing happened."

"Unfortunately." He studied her flushed face, the way she was suddenly fiddling with a chipped nail and evading his eyes. "I hope I didn't upset you."

"What's to be upset about?"

"You confided in me."

"A lot of people confide in you."

"Yes. And when they do, I listen, I advise, offer a prayer, then leave it at that. We both know I didn't in this case. If you've got a problem with the way I touched you, I'd like you to tell me."

"Why?" She went very still, then met his gaze. "Conscience bothering you?"

"Not at all." He traced the mouth he still desired in the most intense way. "The reason I asked is because unless you have objections, what didn't happen, will."

"You certainly sound sure of yourself." Her lips moved beneath his fingertip. She made no attempt to break the contact, though her eyes were wary. "Aren't you taking a lot for granted?"

If there was one thing he excelled at, Matthew knew it lay in his ability to sense people out. He drew upon his seasoned skill and honed in on Dee.

She was scared of something. Emotional involvement? Yeah, he'd lay money that she'd been burned. But it was more than that. He pondered the mixed signals she sent: a challenging glare, desirous gaze, and a look that tugged at his heart because it was lost and alone and so poorly masked by bravado. He perceived a woman of depth and heart. One she was doing her best to harden, but without much success.

He didn't have the whole picture, but he grasped enough to know it would take a special man, a patient man, to scale those invisible walls and get close to a woman he concluded would prove well worth the wait.

Matthew nodded knowingly, then walked away.

When he was at the kitchen door she called to him.

"You never answered me, Rev. Peters. What makes you so sure that what didn't happen has a snowball's chance in hell to—"

"I think you know the answer, Dee." Glancing over his shoulder, he tossed her a smile. "It's inside you, where all of them really are."

Dee stared at the vacant doorway for a long time. She didn't want to delve deeply where he'd suggested she find her answers. It was too tender in that region, with her heart betrayed, nearly mangled, and doing its best to limp along until time, perhaps, healed it.

But time was borrowed for a woman on the run. And enigmatic ministers who could make her ache for a kiss, and share his sense of peace and solidity, spelled emotional danger.

Dee suddenly realized she was tracing her lips with a fingertip and pretending it was his. Carefully and quickly, while she dared, she searched that wounded place he'd unexpectedly touched. It still vibrated in response to his nearness, the soothing yet arousing timbre of his voice, but most of all to the moment when he'd made her feel she wasn't alone and her fears bowed to a kind of strength she had never met.

Deciding she'd explored inside more than what was wise, she quickly shut the lid on her heart.

But not before she found an answer that left her stomach churning and her pulse tripping.

Rev. Matthew Peters intended to kiss her, and soon. And that kiss, she was certain, would hold the power to restore some of the faith she'd lost in men.

Three

Dee was grateful for two things: Loren remaining silent during their meal, and her having changed her tank top for a loose cotton blouse. Since the neighborhood grocery closed at six P.M. on Sundays and there was little in the pantry, they'd had no choice but to go out to eat.

The Talk of the Town Restaurant was aptly named, Dee decided, judging from the curious glances sent their way. And Matthew apparently knew the entire population of Hayes, because everyone waved at him. His return wave was then taken as an entree to meet the newest citizens, who were trapped in a booth.

Between introductions Dee concluded *they* were the talk of the town. Everyone was aware of who she was, but they weren't exactly clear about what had drawn her there. They appeared friendly; she had a stiff mouth from forcing smiles. They were curious; she was tired of rambling off pat answers.

Matthew was a godsend throughout the grueling meal. He excelled in his ability to smooth out awkward conversations, usually with a concerned question about this person's health or how that one's corn crop was faring.

"Dessert, kids?" Matt stacked his empty plate on theirs and handed the dishes to the waitress clearing the table. "Darlene always puts extra cherries on the hot fudge sundaes."

"Can I have extra whipped cream too?" Jason looked hopefully at Darlene, who agreed without a pause.

"What about you, Loren?"

"I'm not a kid," she muttered with a surly expression on her face.

"None for Loren, I guess." Matthew appeared not to have taken offense and promptly turned his attention to Dee.

"I don't care for any either," she quickly replied. Dessert would be an hour alone with Matthew. Dessert would be a good-night kiss from him.

"Warm?" He leaned closer and studied her face. "You look a little flushed, Dee. I hope you're not ill."

Reaching across the table, he pressed his palm to her forehead.

"I'm fine, really. It's just a little stuffy in here." Though with her stomach jumping and her head dizzy with sensations, she did wonder if she *was* ill.

"*Suffocating* might better describe it." As quickly as his palm had touched her, it was gone. "You haven't had five uninterrupted minutes since we sat down."

As if to prove his point, another visitor—Mrs. Henderson—came by. "Well, I do declare, if it's not Rev. Matthew." Her very friendly smile perceptibly changed when she regarded his companions. "Oh, my, and he's here with my new neighbors."

As if the old biddy hadn't noticed before she marched her butt over, Dee thought distastefully, but forced a polite nod.

"Then you know Dee and Jason and Loren."

"Yes." Mrs. Henderson eyed Loren's bosom. "Enjoy your stroll today, Loren?"

"Probably as much as you enjoyed hacking your flowers, Mrs. Henderson. Did you know you've got a big black streak on your shirt? Must be from digging in the dirt."

"What?" Mrs. Henderson searched for the stain in earnest. "Where? Where's the dirt?"

"Just kidding." Loren grinned and plucked a cherry from Jason's sundae.

Horrified, Dee glanced at Matthew, silently begging him to intercede because she was beyond speech. Only he was pressing a napkin to his mouth to cover a cough that sounded suspiciously closer to a guffaw.

"Well, I never—" Mrs. Henderson huffed.

"Ahem . . . ah, Sally. About the music for next Sunday . . ." Matt had recovered from his coughing attack, and not a second too soon.

"Yes?" She turned her attention back to him.

"I'd like to drop one of the hymns."

"But we sing only four as it is. We've always sung four. I've been the church pianist for twenty years, and four it's been each and every Sunday."

"Twenty years is a long time without a change in the program. I think we need to try something different."

"Something different?" She sounded as if he'd suggested desecrating the holiest of the holy.

"Sure. I'd like to have everyone get up and move around, mix a little. Greet their neighbors."

"But everyone already knows each other."

"Not necessarily." He nodded in Dee's direction. "And besides, it wouldn't hurt to create an atmosphere of fellowship during the service."

"No disrespect intended, Reverend," Mrs. Henderson said indignantly, "but I've known the people in our church a lot longer than you have, and I say they won't like changing their ways."

"And I say, as pastor, the final decision is mine. We'll try it, and if the congregation doesn't like it, we'll go back to the old format. Nothing wrong with a trial run, is there?"

That shut her up. Dee looked at Matthew with increasing respect. Then he proceeded to demonstrate he wasn't good only at asserting his authority, but could smooth the feathers that were ruffled as a result of it.

"Oh, and by the way, Sally, would you mind playing a solo while everyone else visits?"

"A solo? Of course, I'd be delighted. Is there anything in particular you want, or can I choose?"

"I trust your judgment, Sally. I'm sure you'll select something that will contribute to the spirit of friendship and harmony we want any visitors who might grace our church to feel in our midst."

"I . . . well, yes, of course." With a farewell to Dee and family that was more genial than her greeting, Mrs. Henderson departed.

It was Dee's turn to hide her mouth with a napkin. When Matthew winked, she indulged a throaty chuckle.

"You will visit with us next Sunday, won't you?" he asked.

"After you changed a twenty-year-old tradition in a New York minute?" Dee tapped his shin with her foot while a spark of mischief danced in her eyes. "Reverend, I wouldn't miss that piano solo for the world."

"Sure I can't help with anything before I take off?"

"Positive. You've done so much as it is, I can't thank you enough, Matt. You actually got the kids to bed by nine o'clock, when I was afraid they'd be climbing the walls at midnight. Tomorrow's their first day in a new school and they're wound up tighter than a jack-in-the-box."

So was she. Getting them registered wasn't the cause of her anxiety. All the necessary papers, including the school records she'd gotten a copy of before they left Las Vegas, were ready in her purse. Meeting with the teachers and the prospect of future one-on-one conferences was what she feared.

"They are anxious," Matt agreed. "Loren wanted to know what I thought about the outfit she'd picked out, and Jason asked me to say a prayer that he'd get a teacher who doesn't give homework. I told him I would, but even ministers didn't have the kind of clout he needed to get that one granted."

That quickly he made her forget her worries and smile. A feat that was nothing less than amazing these days. *He* was amazing, she decided, amazingly masculine yet kind and giving.

"Do I want to know what Loren showed you?"

"I doubt it. But she selected something more, shall we say, acceptable, when I mentioned that the particular style she'd chosen had gone out here years ago and baggy was in. Fortunately, she doesn't know I'm fairly new to the area and what I understand about fashion wouldn't take a minute to explain."

"You are a delight, Matthew Peters. Delightfully . . . *devious*."

"I can be. When it serves a good purpose. But I much prefer to be honest, say what I'm really thinking."

"And what are you thinking now?"

"That the flowers Mrs. Henderson brought over would look better on you than this old piano Mrs. Adams wanted out of her basement." Matt picked a daisy out of the vase Dee held and tucked the yellow bloom behind her ear.

"Matches your hair." Next he selected a stalk of vivid blue statice and traced her brow before tickling her nose. "Just the color of your eyes." His regard was intimate.

Not only was he amazing, she realized, he was wildly romantic. Matt Peters was the kind of man a woman could fall for and hit ground zero before she knew she'd dropped.

He was the kind of man a woman in trouble could turn to for support and help.

Dee turned away—for a price. She told herself the loss of his promised kiss was a small thing, nothing really, after the other losses she'd endured. But that was a lie, and lying wasn't her forte. This was yet another sacrifice, one she resented. Resentment ran deep and long in her life, and at the moment she could almost resent Matt for making her want what she couldn't have.

Placing the vase on the upright piano she'd gratefully taken off Mrs. Adams's hands for a song, she fussed with the arrangement, then softly played the C-minor chord. Her gaze remained fixed on the keys.

"I wonder what Mrs. Henderson would think of you using her flowers to flirt with me."

"Is that what you think I'm doing . . . flirting?" When she forced a curt nod, he leaned an elbow on top of the piano and studied her. "*Flirting*, now, that's an interesting concept. Toying. Teasing. Leading someone on. It's not my style, Dee. I prefer a much more direct approach. Or hadn't you noticed?"

What she noticed was that he stood so close his chest nearly brushed her shoulder and his hips all but rubbed against hers. The room seemed to shrink in size while Matthew's presence expanded. His scent, his aura, surrounded her.

She wanted to breathe him in, fill herself up with this man who was unlike any other she'd ever known. Fighting against him, but mostly against herself, she plucked the daisy from her hair and stuck it back into the vase.

"In that case, I doubt Mrs. Henderson would approve of the good Reverend's direct approach with her flowers."

"And you care?" He chuckled. "Especially when you're setting them on a piano that'll likely hurt her quota of students."

"I guess Mrs. Adams told you my line of business too?"

"No, Jason did. He mentioned it to me when I tucked him in."

Dee struggled to keep her voice conversational. "What else did he tell you?"

"Not much. Just that you miss your baby grand and the kids you taught before moving here. And you're the best piano teacher ever and that mean old Mrs. Busybody next door's going to be asking you for lessons herself once she finds out you know more about music than she could in a million years."

Managing a small laugh, Dee trilled two keys to buy enough time to slow the racing of her heart.

"That'll teach me to keep my opinions to myself. I don't think such talk would endear me to my neighbor."

"Youngsters are just honest. Unlike a lot of adults." His pause was significant. "How long have you played?"

"All my life, it seems."

"Did you study anywhere special?"

"My mother taught me." Dee caught herself before she mentioned her Juilliard degree. She wondered if the diploma she'd proudly displayed still hung in her vacated Las Vegas apartment, or if Vince had burned it in one of his rages, just as she'd had to torch all ties to her past. "A lot of what I know is self-taught," she added, improvising. "Life's been a tough teacher. I graduated from the school of hard knocks."

"With honors?" Matt asked softly.

The fraction of an inch he moved in her direction should have been imperceptible, but she sensed it. His nearness stirred her imagination, and she could easily picture his chest brushing her breasts, his tongue flicking into her ear, and his groin riding the side of her hip.

Dee shut her eyes tightly. There was an ache between her thighs, and her breasts tingled. She was shaking from the inside out with such startling intensity, she felt as if she were waking from years of being in a coma. He wasn't even touching her and every nerve end was coming loose, her heartstrings unraveling.

"Did I graduate with honors?" she whispered unevenly. "Let's just say that giving up my piano was not a minor sacrifice. Students are transient, but my piano? I talked to it every morning and kissed it good night. Whenever I was angry I'd pound its keys. Happy, I'd jam and boogie-woogie and run cadences until my fingers were numb."

"And when you were sad?"

"Moonlight Sonata, or Bach. Anything dreary that captured the mood. We shared a lot of feelings, Cristofori and I."

"Cristofori?"

"My piano's name. After the man who crafted the original model." She laughed without humor. "I don't tell many people about our relationship. I mean, they'd think I was crazy. You yourself must believe I'm a little off."

He covered her hand, which was resting on the keys.

"What I believe is that Cristofori was your lover. Maybe for lack of another?"

She stared, unblinking, at the tanned fingers that interlocked with hers. The striking contrast of their skin colors echoed the ivory to ebony keys. His hand rode upon her own as she repeated the melancholy minor chord.

Matthew stroked her third finger down from black to white, lifted it, then pressed. The sweet sound of the major chord filled the silence and lingered before fading.

"Is there a chance you can get Cristofori back?"

"I'm beginning to think anything's possible." Before she could stop herself, she met his searching gaze.

"Anything is possible if you believe strongly enough." His hand left hers, and his fingers, still warm from their shared heat, touched her cheek. "Tell me, Dee, do you believe in things unseen? Like two strangers connecting, both of them a little confused, maybe, because something keeps passing between them that defies reason. Every time they share a look they feel a need to touch, but both pretend it's not happening and they say what's polite and acceptable when more than anything they're aching to kiss. Deeply. Intimately." His head descended, stopping just short of a kiss. "Do you believe?"

She believed that if he kissed her, she would beg for more. Beg this man of quiet power to listen and make right what couldn't be righted without a miracle. She wanted to touch him, feel his hands on her while she spilled out every heartache, every hope, every wide-awake nightmare that composed what had become her existence.

And how long had she known him? Less than a day.

Oh, Dee, how desperate you must be. Desperate enough to sacrifice what you've staked your life on with a near stranger. And it's not just you. Jason and Loren hang on every word out of your mouth, every action you take. Don't do it. Dear God, don't you do it.

"What I believe, Matt, is that it's time you went home."

He kept his face close to hers as he softly stroked her cheek, a feather-light brush that nearly drove her mad with the need to feel his mouth cover her own.

"Know what I believe?" he said huskily. "That leaving is the last thing you really want from me, and I'm dangerously close to compromising my position more than I already have." He stepped back, and she felt his loss too keenly. "I'll see myself out, Dee. By the way, thanks for the best Sunday, the best any day I've had in a long, long time."

The soft click of the front door sounded a moment later. The high-pitched revving of an engine—she couldn't find it possible to believe it was that of a motorcycle—soon purred down the street.

The breath she'd been holding rushed out on a sigh. A smile she didn't mean to smile, but that asserted itself over every reason she had not to, commanded her lips to obey. Just as her fingers refused to acknowledge the message to play Moonlight Sonata.

As Pachelbel's Canon in D filled her ears, Dee felt her heart lift while she murmured two syllables: "Matthew."

Four

"Loren?" Dee rapped on the bathroom door for the second time in half an hour. "Loren, could you please hurry? The pizza party's in twenty minutes, and I need to brush my teeth."

"Aw, jeez, Dee, give me a break."

She'd like to give her a break—right between the choppers. The last few days had been hell, and Loren was the primary cause. Registration had gone smoothly. Their teachers were so warm and wonderful, Dee decided Matt had done considerable praying on their behalf. But two phone calls from the junior high principal had stolen her bliss.

Lipping the homeroom teacher was Loren's first offense. Skipping the resulting detention was her second.

"Your time's up, and I mean it. We have one bathroom and you don't have the monopoly on it, your highness."

The door was flung open. "You used to call me princess."

For a moment Dee allowed herself to remember when. Loren, the most beautiful baby she'd ever seen, the first she'd ever held. A precious, real-live baby doll who cooed sweetly while Dee dressed her up in tiny white frocks. Oh, how she'd loved her little princess and how her little princess had loved her back.

An "easy child" Loren's grandmother had sagely decreed. Where had the easy child gone? Dee knew too well. Loren's father had poisoned everything he touched, choked out the goodness of life and love within the grip of his powerful fist. But knowing Vince was the cause didn't make her angel-turned-hellion any more pleasant to raise, even if it did soften Dee's heart and strengthen her resolve to undo the spoils of his destruction.

Vince. Suave, gorgeous Vince, who'd mesmerized a young girl and that young girl's family. He was rich. Hardworking too, though he'd disguised his dirty dealings with legal trappings. Dee had first met him more than half her lifetime ago, and she could still remember how she'd elevated him to the status of a hero to be worshipped and a dream lover she wished for her own.

In many ways she and Loren had grown up together. One of the reasons, she realized, that Loren didn't easily bow to her authority any more than Dee could stomach what Vince had done to them both. He'd abused the love and trust she had naively given, and he'd corrupted Loren's sweet, easy nature.

Dee's throat tightened. Remembering the good was almost more biting than recalling the bad.

"I miss my princess," she said painfully.

Loren hesitated before hugging Dee. "Me too, Dee. But your princess is gone. Gone with the mother who found out who my father was too late." She shook her head sadly. "I'm really sorry for hurting you in the ways I do. I love you, but I can't help being what I am."

"Yes, you can. We'll always have to look over our shoulders, but we have to go on. If we don't, Vince wins whether he finds us or not."

"I hate him for that. I hate him for everything."

"He's your father, so I shouldn't say it, but Vince is a bad seed. If only I hadn't been so young, I would have seen him for what he was sooner. If only—"

"I hope he burns in hell. He deserves it. Maybe Rev. Matthew can pray it comes true."

"No." Dee gripped her shoulders. "Matt is a fine, and undoubtedly trustworthy person. But even he can't know about your father."

"Vince." Loren spat out the name as if it were a profanity. "I can't wait to grow up and get even."

"We'll never get even, Loren, and that's something we have to accept. But we do have a chance to make a clean break. It's up to us to make the best of it."

"Right, living like we're poor, pretending we're someone we're not, and hiding where no one can connect mine and Jason's last name to cash in. Vince did this to us. He needs to pay."

Dee absorbed the cool hatred in Loren's voice. Despite her efforts to shield the children from the harshest truths, Loren had developed a thirst for vengeance that matched her father's—a sign that she'd gotten them away none too soon.

"You used to call him Daddy," Dee said gently, hoping to temper the unhealthy attitude.

"Yeah, well, I quit calling him that before you stopped calling me princess. Besides, Jason and I always called you Dee, and you're a lot more of a mother to us than he ever was a father."

"Hearing you say that means a great deal to me." Dee held Loren as tightly as the secrets that bound them. "I know it's hard, what we're going through, but you could help us all by staying out of trouble at school."

"Okay, Dee. I'll serve my detention tomorrow. And I'll really try to be good."

"You *are* good. No matter what happens, don't forget it."

Loren pulled away and fixed Dee with a mature gaze. "Forgetting's not easy. But I'll do my best to try."

"For Mama?"

"Yes, Dee. For Mama. For you. For anyone but Vince."

Throughout the pizza party Loren was the princess Dee remembered. Jason was, well, Jason, which was perfectly fine, *and* energy consuming. But Matthew was . . . not himself.

He was polite. Too infuriatingly polite. He wasn't the flesh and blood man who had recently bid her good night and left her hungering for his kisses.

"I'm so glad you decided to join us tonight, Dee," he said pleasantly. So damn pleasantly she could have been someone he'd just met. "I hope you and the kids had a good time."

"Sure did, Rev. Matthew." Jason patted his stomach. "That was awesome pizza."

"I liked the rap music." Loren studied the tips of her shoes as if she were embarrassed to admit she'd enjoyed herself, even though it was obvious, since they were the last to leave. "Thanks for inviting us."

"Anytime, Loren. By the way, how's school?"

"Okay, I guess." Darting a glance at Dee, who smiled encouragingly, she cut off further conversation by tugging at Jason's arm. "C'mon, bro. Let's go home."

"Nah, I'll wait for Dee."

"Scared of the dark?" Loren glanced from one

adult to the other, then slipped Dee a sly smile. "What a woose."

"I'm not a woose!"

"Are too." With that she turned for the basement doors. Jason was fast on her heels, leaving with a quickly muttered, "Thanks, Rev. Matt."

"I knew it was too good to last." Dee shook her head while stifling a chuckle. Loren's ploy to leave the grown-ups alone was so obvious, even Jason should have seen through it. Certainly it wasn't lost on a minister who was suddenly shoving his hands into his pockets and focusing his attention on the swishing doors.

"Getting settled all right?" he asked in a stilted tone.

"Fine." Before he'd begun acting so impersonal, she would have been tempted to share her less than fine conversations with Loren's principal. Maybe keeping the distance was better. Only it didn't feel better. It felt terrible.

"Loren certainly seems to be adjusting well."

"I think, hope, she's trying to clean up her act."

"Good for her."

"It's good for me too," Dee said with feigned lightness.

"Yes, yes. I'm sure it is."

"Speaking of cleaning up, why don't I help you with this before I leave?"

"There's really no need. Just a few trash bags to take out, some cups to pick up. I can manage that."

"But I insist." Why wouldn't he look at her? Had she sprouted an extra eyeball? And why did he seem so eager to get away from her when three nights before he'd been anything but? "After all your help, it's the least I can do, Matt."

He did look at her then. A fleeting glance that rocked the floor beneath her high heels. Wearing a slim skirt and delicate gauze blouse, she'd dressed tastefully but with an eye toward pleasing a man. She'd told herself she was doing it only for herself, to buoy her lagging self-confidence. Self-confidence that had taken a great fall when Matthew hadn't seemed to notice.

He seemed to notice now. His fleeting glance was filled with raw, undiluted masculine attraction. A hungry look. One that said he'd like to gobble her up so fast, he wouldn't have time to savor a single, delectable bite.

Yummy, she decided. He was the yummiest man she'd ever met and being devoured by Rev. Matthew Peters was the most appetizing fantasy she could imagine.

"I'll take care of the cups," Dee said happily. "I saw some sponges in the kitchen and I'll wipe off the tables too."

He made an inarticulate sound she took as a "go ahead." Dee could feel his gaze hot upon her back as she moved down several long tables, gathering paper cups.

While she hummed softly, Matthew made a lot of noise pounding trash bags, she noticed. She took her time wiping the tables, wanting these stolen moments to last. When he stopped causing a ruckus, she glanced furtively at him and saw that he was staring at her as if making up for his earlier abstinence.

And if she leaned too far over the table, causing her skirt to stretch tightly across her behind, who could blame her? Her ego was suffering from neglect, due to circumstances that made the state of one's ego a trivial matter.

Dee could feel her cheeks growing warm. She could hardly believe her own actions, albeit subtle. And effective, judging from Matt's tense posture, the grinding of his teeth, and tortured cast to his gaze, which he jerked away when she turned to him with an innocent smile.

"Anything else I can do?" Dee said sweetly.

"I think you've done enough." His reply was gruff. And the way he hauled a black sack in each clenched fist spoke of fierce emotion.

"I'll hold the door open for you." The click-click-click of her heels echoed over the linoleum tile. The ragged sound of Matt's breathing ended with a whoosh when he brushed past her and his flexed arm grazed her left breast.

Now, *that* she hadn't intended. Reflexively, Dee crossed her arms as heat seeped through her. She could feel exactly where he had touched.

"Sorry," he said hoarsely. He paused. His clenched jaw worked back and forth before he tilted it in her direction. His look was brief but incisive. She flushed with giddy pleasure because it told Dee the only thing he was sorry about was that he was gripping the bags instead of her.

She'd never seen a man move so fast. He had the bags deposited on the curb and the church key in his hand before she'd recovered from his silent message.

"Get your purse and I'll walk you home."

Actually, it was closer to a trot. Dee almost had to run to keep up with his agitated stride. But she refused to vault over the steps to her porch as he did.

"Thank you for a lovely evening, Matt," she said, winded. He didn't look at her but stared at a point above her head, close to the yellow bug light. "We all had a wonderful time."

"Great." For being such a sincere guy, he didn't sound too honest at the moment.

"Matthew, is something wrong?"

Very slowly he lowered his gaze until his eyes locked with hers. The force of the meeting made

Dee step back. When he continued to simply stare without answering, she extended her hand. His eyes shifted to it, but he remained still, as if he were debating the merits of exercising protocol.

Just as she was about to make the decision for him by stepping inside the house and slamming the door shut in his face, Matt accepted her offering. A streak of electric sensation passed between them, and Dee's arm jerked. The current was strong enough to zap them both to kingdom come.

He didn't shake her hand, though she felt a distinct tremble in their grip. Then he firmly enfolded her hand in his and his thumb raked seductively back and forth over her knuckles until a small, muffled moan escaped her. They stared at each other's mouths while their joined hands stroked and fondled in a parody of mad, passionate lovemaking.

When the front door banged open, they sprang apart as if caught in the act. Loren looked at them with the tsk-tsk expression of a chaperon.

"I was afraid you were locked out, Dee." She pushed out the screen door until it rested against the exterior wall.

Right, Dee thought. *And that grin on your face is just about as discreet as your setup to get us alone.*

"Guess I'd better shove off." Matthew rubbed his palms together and Dee wondered if he was stalling for time or wiping off the sweat they'd worked up. "Hope you can make it on Sunday."

"We'll be there. Front row. Count on it."

"I will." His smile was quick and easy—the smile she had missed more than she wanted to admit when he'd kept it from her all night after she'd dreamed about it for days.

"Till Sunday, then." Four days. Four days too many.

"Guess I'd better shove off."

"You said that already." Loren tapped her foot in time to the drumming of her fingers on the door frame.

Both adults turned on her with glaring eyes. "Good night, Loren," they said in unison.

"Good night, Rev. Matthew. I'll wait up for you in the kitchen, Dee." She spun around and went back inside.

Matthew chuckled. Dee threw up her hands and laughed.

"Loren left the door open," she noted.

"Both of them. Think she's trying to tell us something?"

"Maybe just a subtle hint." Dee inhaled the fresh breeze. It carried Matthew's scent and she responded to it unconsciously. She leaned against the wall and peered at him through half-closed lids. "I haven't been waited up for in years."

He moved in closer, until his palms rested on either side of her head and his face descended, then stopped scant inches from hers. His breath, warm and fragrant, fanned her even warmer face.

"Maybe Loren doesn't trust me."

"Even Loren knows I should be safe with a minister."

"I'm also a man." Reaching around the frame, he switched off the porch light. They were suddenly cloaked in darkness. And in that darkness she felt the pressure of his thumbs rotating slowly against her temples. "A minister might be safe, Dee, but don't overestimate the protection my profession affords you. I have only so much restraint, and last Sunday exhausted a good deal of my supply."

There was a distinct edge of warning in his softly spoken words. An unexpected flavor of danger relayed itself in the increasing pressure of his massage. Running for her life had sent her to the most remote town she could find, so yes, she was well acquainted with the adrenaline rush of fear. But her too-rapid heartbeat was closer to a forbidden thrill.

"You're breathing fast," he whispered. "Wonder why?"

"Are you going to kiss me?"

His low chuckle was a seductive rumble. "It's all I've been able to think about since the last time I saw you."

"You didn't act like it tonight."

His fingertips stroked up her throat, then framed her jaw.

"I can act like a lot of things, and one of them's not being a minister—especially since it's the shorter of my careers. Make that callings."

"You mean that you haven't always pastored a church?"

"I have a college degree in philosophy, another degree from a seminary. And yes, I've pastored a church before this. But I've spent more time in other pursuits. Curious yet?"

"Very. Tell me, who *is* Matthew Peters?"

"If you really want to know, tell me more about Dee Sampson," he said softly. "Where does she come from, why is she here, and what's in her past that brings her to the present . . . on a front porch waiting for, rather than taking, a kiss from me? Did some man teach you differently, Dee?"

"What man?" she asked quickly, her guard rising.

"You tell me. There was a man, wasn't there? My guess is he's one who liked to call the shots, and didn't appreciate a woman who strikes me as independent but alone. An intriguing woman I want to know much better. A deal, Dee. Tell me about you and I'll return the favor equally."

Dee stiffened, suddenly aware of the potential foolishness of acting on her desires. Matt had lulled her into a sense of security and she'd heedlessly thrown caution to the wind. His words hit too close to home. Did he know Nick? Or Vince? The two men who'd ruled her life had contacts that extended to politicians, law officials, even coroners. A minister—who admitted to pursuing other endeavors and didn't fit the stereotype—wasn't out of the realm of possibility.

"You go first, Matt. Who *are* you?" she demanded.

"A man. A man with a mission who's made mistakes along the way and doesn't want to foul things up with you. Now it's your turn. Turnabout is fair play, and ministers are inclined to like things fair, you know."

He liked things fair? Did he actually consider tracing her lips with the faintest brush of the tip of his tongue and gliding his chest like a whisper over her breasts *fair*? She didn't believe he was Vince's man; her sharpened instincts for survival said he was not. What they did say was that the Matt beneath the clergyman's cloth could be far more hazardous than Sunday's encounter had let on.

She began to edge away. "I think I'd better go in."

"I think not." He deftly trapped her between his braced arms. "Tell me, is running away a habit of yours?"

"No more than bribing is yours," she shot back. "And as for running, that was quite a dash you made out of church to get me home. You make me uneasy, Reverend, the way you change colors faster than clothes."

"Ah, nice volley. But since you put it back in my court, I'll explain, which is more than I'm getting from you. The truth is, I was trying to give you the space you wanted last Sunday. I was afraid you thought I used my position to take advantage of yours. But if anyone was taking advantage tonight, it was you."

"I was not!"

"No?" His fingertips scaled her ribs, then cinched her waist. "Somehow I couldn't help but notice the way you kept bending over after making sure I was watching. Quite an eyeful you gave me in that short skirt. Really, Dee, trying to tempt a minister like that, actually enjoying yourself at my expense. Do you think I'm so holy that I haven't imagined a dozen ways I'd like to make you pay up?"

"What I think is that this game is over."

"Game over? It never was a game, Dee. At least, not for me." His face was a hair's breadth away from hers, and his hips were so close his legs would be straddling her own if he moved an inch toward her. "Do you still want that kiss?"

Did she still want that kiss? More than ever— and that was the danger, because, as she was beginning to realize, Matthew Peters didn't flirt or play games and he had more facets than a gemstone. She turned her head to the side, saying, "What I want is a reason for your still being here."

"That's simple. I like you. I care about you. In fact, I care enough to risk showing you a side of my human nature that few people see." His arm brushed hers as he reached for the switch. Dee blinked against the sudden light. And then she blinked against Matthew's impassioned gaze. "You're awfully quiet now. Cat got your tongue, Dee?" he whispered. "Lucky kitty, if he does."

Her jaw went slack. Her tongue danced against her teeth. And her mind did contortions trying to sort him out. What kind of a man could say such things at the same time his eyes softened and his lips pressed gently against her forehead?

If she didn't stop him now, she feared he might work his way down. She put a palm to his chest and pushed.

"Back off, Matt . . . please." Much to her disappointment, he did. He turned to leave but unwisely, she didn't want him to go and caught his arm. "I don't understand you. And as much as I wish that I did, I'm not certain I should."

"There's a lot I wish I understood too, Dee. Like where you've been and where we're going. Be glad that I'm searching for answers rather than demanding them and making you lose more faith."

"I suppose you mean faith in my fellow man?"

"Exactly. You admitted yours was shaken, and if you really want to grasp where I'm coming from, ask yourself this: How many men would expose their true concerns and flaws before taking a kiss or more from that luscious mouth of yours? Think about it, Delilah."

She did. Battling against her confusion and the arousal he'd summoned without so much as a kiss, she did think.

"Not many," she finally admitted.

"I'm glad you realize that. Just be aware that I'm not always as admirable as I strive to be."

"Is that a warning, Rev. Peters?"

"It is. I want you to trust me, and for that reason I'd best keep my distance until you can."

He removed her firm grip on his arm, then kissed her hand in a way that was sweet, almost courtly—until she felt the flick of his tongue and the graze of teeth against knuckles. She drew in a sharp breath, and her inner thighs quivered. When he briefly pressed his hips against hers, she felt the straining in his pants.

"See what I mean?" he said, then turned around

and left. She stared after him even as he disappeared into the darkness.

Dee saw exactly what he meant. Matthew Peters, man of inner strength and apparently a few secrets of his own, deemed it wise to keep his distance because he didn't trust himself.

Which only made her trust him that much more.

Five

Was something wrong? she'd asked him on the porch Wednesday night. Was something wrong? Hell, yes, something was wrong! When he spent Saturday afternoon on his motorcycle tearing up the road instead of preparing the next morning's sermon, something was definitely wrong.

Gravel spewed in the wake of Matthew's tires as he leaned into a sharp curve. He hadn't taken his two-wheeled baby for this kind of spin since he left his biker gang more than six years earlier. They still kept in touch, though, and had a loose date for next spring. He couldn't help but imagine what kind of reception fifty motorcycles and their tattooed owners would get upon a visit to his church.

A vision of Sally Henderson banging out the doxology over the roar of engines and old Maude choking on a hymn while the bikers filed down the aisles left him howling with laughter.

He needed to laugh. If he laughed, maybe he could keep from thinking about Dee and the internal havoc he was wrestling with. As it turned out, even laughter didn't help.

Two steps forward, three steps back with her. He was feeling the beat, but it beat the hell out of him how to guide the speed. Was it him, he wondered. Was he still so burned out from the homeless mission that he was screwing up somehow, making the wrong calls, or, worst of all, misreading her role in his life?

Was Dee the one he'd been waiting for? Was that why just the thought of her caused his blood to rush, his head to spin, and his heart to flip-flop? He'd indulged in many affairs during his break from the ministry, but they'd only met his physical needs and nothing else.

Slowing his mad race to a Sunday ride and then a halt, he parked his cycle beside a deserted road, then sat beneath an old maple tree.

A cornfield stretched endlessly across the graveled street. His past seemed to stretch just as endlessly behind him. And the future? It was infinite, full of possibilities and pitfalls when he craved certainties and absolute answers.

"Look," he said, gazing up to the sky, "last Sunday was a real treat, even if it was a little hard on the moral check and balance system. But Wednesday was a sure sign I'm dangerously short in the control department. Quite frankly, these past few days have been the devil. I'm getting uncomfortably toasty just thinking about facing that front pew tomorrow."

Matthew shut his eyes and listened. At least he tried to listen. With all the mayhem going on in his head, he was having trouble hearing. Or maybe he simply didn't want to take the chance of being called on the carpet for what he'd been thinking.

With a weary sigh he looked around him, drawing strength from the beauty that the Lord had made. Well, He'd made him too, with a little help from his parents. Only Matthew didn't want to think about them any more than he wanted to keep going over the situation with Dee. He did anyway.

He was human. He was a man. One who was trying to juggle his calling and responsibilities and earthy nature which had never asserted such a fierce hold.

Had he ever lusted? Many times. Had he ever indulged temptation's offerings? Oh, yes. Only to regret it because he'd felt reduced, more isolated in his path, and yearning for what was lasting, deep, and real.

Lasting. Deep. Real. Such were the kind of problems he intuited Dee faced. He was in a position to help her, whatever form that took. And yet, how could he act effectively as counselor while he was aching with the need to have her?

Truth? He wanted sex with her. Get-down, hot and heavy, any way the imagination could conceive, *sex.* He wanted it bad. He wanted it good. He wanted more.

To honor her body and join their spirits. To win her trust and for once in his life have someone *he* could confide in and draw strength from when the burden became too heavy. A soulmate on earth he could turn to so he'd have more than prayer as a companion.

The sun was dipping low in the sky when Matthew unzipped his light jacket and withdrew a well-thumbed Bible. He touched the treasured inscription on the first page.

For Matthew. Our son and God's. We've always been proud of you but never prouder than on this day of your graduation from the seminary. We thank you for sharing your life with us as you do so generously with others. May peace and love always be yours. Dad and Mom.

Matthew shook his head. In the near decade that had passed since he'd received this, his parents had had cause to retract their words. Peace and love had not always been his after all.

Earnestly, he began searching the thin, delicate pages for what peace he could find.

"As you'll notice in the church bulletin, we're forgoing the usual hymn to take the opportunity to share in fellowship. Don't be shy. You don't have to whisper or stay glued to your pew. Stretch your legs and share your hearts. And handshakes are good too."

Scattered laughter echoed through the quaint church. Matthew raised his hands, which hadn't been this damp since he'd delivered his first sermon. "Please rise and let's greet one another with joy, for on this beautiful new day we're blessed to be living."

Before he could nod to Sally, the sound of an elaborate composition filled the hallowed halls.

A quick observation assured him that the congregation was closer to running with the ball than dropping it. Carefully allocating his attention to the members of the gathering, he moved from pulpit to flock.

At the front pew Dee and Loren and Jason had their backs turned to him as people pumped their hands. Matt struggled not to remember the erotic manipulations he and Dee had devised in a moment of restrained passion. He'd been struggling not to remember a lot of things in the last fifteen minutes, which seemed closer to fifteen hours.

Relieved to pass Dee's row, he moved down the aisles, shaking hands and returning greetings by rote. Just when he thought he could actually pull off reversing directions and retreating to some safety behind the pulpit, Jason waved at him. Dee, who was busy acknowledging Maude's welcome, glanced his way.

Their eye-to-eye contact was brief but significant.

She'd challenged him in a millisecond stare.

With a deep breath Matthew confronted the unavoidable.

"Have you met the church's new neighbors?" Maude patted Loren on the back and was rewarded with a tight, forced smile. "This is Loren and this is Jason and this is—"

"We've all met, thanks, Maude. How are you, bud?" Matt focused hard on Jason. "Nice suit you're wearing today."

"I didn't want to wear it, but Aunt—"

"Aunt Hazel sent it for his birthday, and she'll be pleased to hear it fits so well. Won't she, Jason?" The color in Dee's cheeks ran high. Her voice was higher than usual too, and softly breathless.

"Yes, Dee. That's right."

Now that he'd been forced to listen to her voice and look directly at her face instead of over her head, Matthew couldn't take his eyes off Dee. Maude was rambling on about last week's family reunion, but he tuned her out while Dee turned him on with no more than her hesitant smile.

"And you're all invited to the pot luck lunch after church. Right, Rev. Matthew? *Ahem*. Rev. Matthew. I *said* they should join us for lunch, right?"

"Oh, yes. Yes, of course, Maude."

Matthew was distantly aware that Sally was going into her grand finale.

"That's a lovely piece Mrs. Henderson is playing. A very impressive solo." Dee gestured toward the piano.

Allowing himself the luxury of sharing their private joke, Matthew smiled. "I think that's the general idea."

The stained glass window to her side cast a glow over the smooth and infinitely touchable texture of her skin. His fingers tingled, remembering the feel of it. Before he was consciously aware of the action, he lifted his hand to touch her once again.

"Guess I'd better get back to the choir loft."

Maude's voice broke into his trance. What was he thinking, doing? In front of God was one thing, in front of the entire congregation was another matter entirely.

His hand poised between him and Dee, he covered the awkward lapse by reaching for Dee's hand in what he hoped appeared to be a welcoming gesture.

Sssssss. He could have been testing a hot iron with a licked finger. Dee's breath audibly caught. His own was compressed into a groan that lodged in his throat.

Caught between the urge to haul her into his arms and cut off his own before he did it, Matthew somehow managed to extricate himself from their melded grip.

His heart was laboring by the time he climbed the few steps back to the pulpit.

"Let us pray," he said in a hoarse voice. He prayed for strength. He prayed for guidance. He prayed for inner peace and good judgment. He prayed as he'd never prayed before in his life. *Amen.*

After the collection plate was passed and announcements made, Matthew reluctantly relinquished his nice padded chair to approach the pulpit once more. He was careful not to look directly at Dee, afraid he'd go blank if he did.

"Friends, I have a story I'd like to share with you."

Good, he told himself, good. Voice even, hands no longer sweating. There went little Andy scribbling in the hymnal. There went Andy's mom yanking it away and pinching his chubby thigh. Business as usual, he thought. Matthew launched into his sermon, satisfied he could pull it off.

"We're all familiar with tax collectors, aren't we?" He surveyed the nodding heads. "And everyone knows what a scarlet woman is, certainly." Several of the heads quit nodding and turned in a single direction. Matthew automatically followed their path.

Dee. He'd known some small minds hadn't been overly accepting of her presence, but he'd had no idea the gossip had gotten so mean. It was too late to revise his opening, but at least Matthew could thank heaven that she was in the front pew and appeared unaware of the eyes boring into the back of her head. Anger, immediate and forceful, had him gripping the pulpit tightly.

But that wasn't all that had him clenching and unclenching his hands.

She was bathed in a golden glow. Her eyes, luminous and sparkling, were fixed on his mouth. He wet his lips and groped for the words that had vacated his brain.

"These, uh, people were, um, social outcasts. Judged and—and condemned by moralists who thought themselves righteous enough to . . . play God."

Matthew jerked his gaze away and stared down the same breed of moralists addressed in his sermon. He'd intended to speak of the wrongness in prejudging others, but now he was fueled by outrage that such unjust prejudice had been visited upon Dee and her family.

In the face of his silence, the church was unnaturally quiet. And then there was a low murmur which he broke with a voice unlike his usual pleasant tone, one that was stern and challenging. Once Matthew had the eyes that had turned on Dee glued to the floor, he continued his message, subtly making his point by using the viewpoint of those shunned.

Afterward at the pot luck lunch, Matthew stood at the head of the food-laden table and greeted those in line.

"Powerful sermon, Rev. Matthew."

"Thank you, Alice," he replied.

"That was real food for thought you delivered, Pastor," Mr. Fields told him. "Thank you for reminding us of those truths we tend to forget."

"I'm always speaking to myself as much as to the next man, but I'm glad you got so much out of the message."

"What do you think, Rev. Matthew?" Sally Henderson asked excitedly.

What do I think? My blood pressure's still so high it's boiling, the woman I've possibly been waiting for all my life but whom I can't get within ten feet of without touching is next in line, and I'm not up to fighting the no-win battle with an audience at lunch.

"What do I think about what, Sally?"

"About the greeting time. I do believe the congregation liked it after all."

"Yes, I have to agree. I'm sure that beautiful solo you played had a lot to do with encouraging the spirit of fellowship during our worship hour."

"Your message was very thought-provoking, Matthew." Dee didn't offer her hand as had those preceding her. Matt thanked God for small favors.

"That was really neat, the way you pretended you were those Bible people," Jason exclaimed. "Totally cool."

"Yeah," Loren said. "Especially when you tried to talk like that sleazy chick those dumb stone throwers caught getting it on with her boyfriend in a tent. But what I don't understand is why they didn't jump on him too."

"Loren!" Dee gasped.

"I'm glad it kept your attention, Loren. And as

for your question, let's just say we've come a long way, baby."

"Will you sit with us at lunch, Rev. Matt?" Jason asked. "We'd really like that. Especially Dee."

"Jason!" Dee glanced around as her cheeks turned a pretty shade of pink.

"Well, you would. And after everyone's finished eating, would you pass the football with me again, Rev—"

"That's enough, Jason," Dee broke in. "Rev. Matthew has other people besides us to visit with. Come on, kids. Others are waiting to talk to their pastor." She all but shoved her brood forward as she muttered, "Later, Matt."

Dee ended the last note of the Moonlight Sonata and went straight into a morose Bach fugue. With each ponderous chord she remembered Matthew's evasion at lunch. With each mournful measure she relived his stilted apology to Jason for having other duties to attend to, then kindly promising that they'd burn some pigskin again real soon.

As hard as she tried to forget with the rare aid of a bottle of wine, her mind replayed the bitter pill she'd swallowed, smiling all the while she'd cried bitter tears inside. Now she was alone, so damn alone and refusing to let them flow.

Dee could picture how every chance glance they shared was broken by his abrupt turn of the head. Then whenever she moved in his direction he had gone the opposite way and struck up a conversation with anyone but her.

He'd avoided her with such obvious maneuvers that she'd felt like a leper. One of the very outcasts he'd championed in his sermon. And she was one, wasn't she? She'd felt the false acceptance of fleeting cordialities. She'd endured the unspoken scrutiny and the gossip she'd heard whispered behind her back. Dee was still stunned. Stunned and hurt.

Why hadn't she realized? Matthew had a reputation to maintain, a congregation to please, and she apparently struck out on both accounts. He'd given her warnings and explanations that she'd been an idiot not to understand. His interest in her was relegated to clandestine advances on dark porches and in the privacy of a kitchen.

"You bastard," she croaked. "You two-faced bastard. I've been betrayed, my heart nearly torn out. I've been lied to and buried people I've loved. But never have I felt the kind of shame I went through today. You hippocrite, you—"

Laying her head against the piano, Dee vowed she would not, *would not* let go of the sob. She'd choke on it first.

"Cristofori, Cristofori. I miss you so much. I miss you almost as much as I miss Alexis and no one misses her as much as I do." Dee buried her face in her hands.

She was sick of her life. She'd been sick of it for years. Didn't she have enough on her empty platter before one of God's messengers made it his mission to make her life more miserable than it already was?

Deciding she was close to blasphemy and knowing she had enough marks against her as it was, Dee smashed the keys in frustration, then mentally apologized for her disrespect.

"Believe me, I relate," she said to the piano. "I give everything I have to give and no matter how much, it's never half enough."

If only she could escape in sleep and put the whole horrible day, the even more horrible past five years, behind her. But even after downing half a bottle of wine since the kids had gone to bed, she wasn't close to being sleepy.

Hot bubble baths were good for insomnia. So was more wine. Only the more she soaked, and the more wine she drank, the more her mental defenses dissolved. Each bubble seemed a caress tantalizing her sensitized skin. Each sip of wine flowing down her throat created the heady sensation she'd felt when Matthew had traced his fingertips down her neck.

"It's not him," she insisted stubbornly. "Not that prude with the multiple personality disorder. The only reason he's gotten to you, Dee Sampson, is that you haven't let a man touch you in nearly five years. A dog could lick your ankle and probably get the same reaction."

She hiccupped. What was that old remedy, the one about holding liquid in your mouth until the hiccups went away? The first time didn't work, but the second one did. By then she'd forgotten the reason she'd polished off the bottle.

"Uh-oh." Dee giggled tipsily. "All gone." Then she giggled some more. For not being much of a drinker, she'd sure done her share tonight.

Good thing the kids were asleep. She had an example to set. Responsibilities to take care of. She was a damn good mom, but even damn good moms needed down time.

Water sloshed from the tub as she crawled out over the side. Once she'd made it to her feet, Dee pouted at the steamed-up full-length mirror attached to the door. Not a bad body. Not so much as a stretch mark.

She struck a naughty pose, thrusting her breasts out and slowly rotating her flared hips. Flat tummy too. *Humph.* The good Reverend probably thought she wore a girdle. Pursing her lips, she pretended to blow him a kiss.

"Take that, you sanctimonious saint," she said, her words slurred. "C'mon, lover, fall from grace and join me."

Dee wrapped a towel around her, then wove dizzily to her tiny bedroom. The few nightclothes she owned were practical, except for one revealing crimson nightie she could blame only on her hasty packing. She felt it slither like a second skin down her body. It was purchased for a honeymoon, but if she counted the number of times she'd worn it, the gown was still new.

The wisp of silk wasn't enough to suit her sultry mood. She walked to the living room and selected a CD from the few she'd bought with carefully allocated pennies. For her solitary night of debauchery one piece of music was appropriate: Ravel's *Bolero.*

She slid it into Loren's portable player, a garage-sale find, and set it on instant replay. Next she lit some candles. At least ten, and who cared if they burned down to puddles of wax.

Deciding to get drunk, so roaring drunk she'd likely swear off drinking the next morning, Dee got another bottle and set it amid the candles. Just as she stabbed the corkscrew into the cork, she heard a tap. At first she thought it was the music. But then the tapping became more insistent.

Someone was at the door.

Dee froze, sobering up fast. She needed a gun. Why the hell didn't she own a gun? If Vince or Nick or one of their colleagues weren't out there, she was taking a trip this week to an out-of-town pawn shop.

But right now she had to find out if her late-night caller was friend or foe. The only thing she could find for protection was the baseball bat Jason had left by the couch. Hoisting it over her head, she positioned herself beside the front door while her ears picked up the sound of heavy footsteps moving away. She flicked on the porch light.

"Who's there?" she demanded, not having the

benefit of a peephole. The footsteps again, reversing to her direction. "Who's there?" she repeated.

"Dee?" came the answer. "Dee, it's Matthew. I know it's late, but if you'll let me in I—please, Dee. We need to talk. It's important."

Six

Her relief was enormous. She dropped the bat and readily opened the door.

"Matthew. What are you doing here this time of night?"

"I know it's late, and I apologize for that. In fact, there's something else I want to apologize for. Do you think I could come in?"

She was more than happy to oblige. His presence gave her a sense of protection. Her heart was still pounding from fear; it pounded even harder with Matthew's nearness. She suddenly felt light-headed, adrenaline mixed with alcohol coursing through her.

"You came to apologize?" She could give forgive him anything at the moment, she was so grateful he wasn't the predator she'd anticipated.

"Yes, I did. About today—" His speech came to a halt. Matthew blinked. Then he blinked again. "Were you expecting someone?" He looked at her strangely.

"Expecting someone?" she repeated, confused.

His brows drew together. The eyes beneath were unreadable as they moved down from her face to her throat to bare feet, then back up before looking over her shoulder and taking in the living room.

Dee glanced over her own shoulder, almost expecting a freak show from the peculiar expression etched into his strained features. The living room was the same as it had been minutes before. Plain. Humble. And quite cozy thanks to the flickering candles.

"I seem to have come at an inopportune time. Candles. Music. And that"—he cleared his throat—"that thing you're poured into. I also see a fresh bottle of wine. Did I get here before the first cork flew?"

Dee pressed her fingers over her lips to stifle another hiccup. Her immediate disbelief of what he was implying coincided with the need to plead innocent. But something stopped her. Pride? Offense? The sudden inner shout of "What gives him the right after shunning me at lunch?" Perhaps a little twinge of wanting to get even with Matt since she couldn't with anyone else. She decided she wasn't ready to absolve his earlier behavior after all.

"You forgot something, didn't you?" she said coolly. "Like the stud I stashed under my bed so the good minister wouldn't find out that I'm as disreputable as the adultress he sermonized about today? Jason's got a rock collection in his room, if you want to cast a few stones, Reverend."

Even in the muted lighting she could see him flush. "That was uncalled for, Dee."

"And your tacky insinuations weren't?"

"I was simply making an observation."

"An observation distinctly tinged with disapproval."

When he scanned the living room once more, as if to satisfy himself she was alone, Dee felt her ire rise. He wasn't giving her the benefit of the doubt.

"If you're wearing this nightgown for another

visitor," he replied slowly, "you're right. I don't approve."

She rather liked the fact that he disapproved. And it was kind of fun, even interesting, to see Matt off balance for a change. Especially since he'd been jerking her emotions around from day one. Giving in to the less admirable side of her nature, Dee decided to toy with him a bit before setting his mind at ease.

"But surely you realize, Matt, that I wear something like this only when I'm expecting someone."

Her deliberate taunt scored quite a reaction, she noticed with satisfaction. He looked as if an elbow had been planted in his solar plexus. Then his fists clenched and his face hardened, as if he'd like to rip the offending garment right off her and was ready to break any other man's hands that so much as tried.

"Who? Who are you expecting?" he demanded. "Is it an old lover or a new one? Tell me straight, Dee. Right now."

"Why don't you stick around and find out?" She couldn't believe what she was saying. An alarm inside her told her she was courting trouble, but still she went on. "Maybe you can pick up a few pointers on the art of misbehaving."

Dee ran her palms provocatively down her ribs and settled her hands on her hips. Her stance was deliberately sexy. Matthew's gaze heated up several degrees as he followed the movement. Dee liked that so much it made her glad she was woozy enough to do and say things she would be horrified about later. But later was later. This was now, and if she was going to play the scarlet woman, she was doing it with style.

"What's wrong, Rev. Peters? Haven't you ever misbehaved before? No, of course not. Heaven forbid that you tarnish your virtuous soul."

"I've misbehaved plenty in my lifetime," he said flatly.

"Are you bragging or just communing with a sinner before you try to make me see the light and repent for my evil ways?" Throwing herself into the role with zest, she experienced an unexpected exhilaration instead of the shame she should have felt. The dutiful mom was suddenly a bad girl. A temptress. She'd never been a temptress before. The power that came with the new role was a heady rush. Dee pouted prettily, then licked her lips.

"Try to make you repent when you're enjoying yourself so much? Thanks, but I'll save my breath. And as for bragging, it's not something I do, especially about things I'm not particularly proud of. Though you seem quite proud of yourself at the moment. Looks like I grossly overestimated you, Dee. I took you for a woman who sets a good example for her kids instead of one who struts her stuff for kicks before the someone she's expecting even shows."

Dee's spine stiffened. He'd actually bought it! Her baiting had begun as a get-even joke, but she found nothing amusing in his quick acceptance of it.

"Leave my kids out of this, Matthew," she snapped, all play gone now that he'd hit a tender nerve. She wanted to strike back. "You have no right, do you hear me, *no right* to pass judgment on those children or the way I'm raising them. Just keep your high and mighty opinions to yourself."

"Then cover your ears if you don't want to listen, because I have something to say and I'm not leaving until it's out." He spoke with a genuine concern that even in her agitated state she couldn't totally resent. Silently she followed him into the living room.

"Your kids are good kids, but they need stability, a wholesome influence. Jason's starved for attention, a man's attention. And as for Loren, if someone doesn't take a firm hand soon, she's going to be another statistic on the runaway list. Unless she gets pregnant first and ends up with a baby when she's still a child herself, as her mother did." He gestured to the candles, the wine, the CD player spilling out sultry music, and shook his head. "Look around you, Dee. They don't need this kind of environment. Even if you do."

His concern twisted her insides into a knot. He wanted her; in his eyes she saw that. He thought her capable of promiscuity and still he wanted her and worried about her children's welfare. Yet another facet of this enigma who was more confusing and compelling than ever.

He really got to her, as no one ever had. But men had put her through hell—including Matt—and she needed to find out just how deep his waters ran. She wanted to see him in all his colors and flaws, stripped to the bone without a stitch of control.

"And I suppose you care?" she said flippantly.

"Hell yes, I care."

"You have a strange way of showing it, Rev. Peters."

He stared at her, incredulous. "I have treated you with respect and concern."

"Have you now? Coming into my house in the middle of the night and passing judgment not only on my child-rearing techniques, but on how I choose to spend my free time, hits me another way."

"I'll tell you how it hits me. If spending your free time includes dressing up in the likes of skimpy nightgowns and waiting up for a cheap thrill, I've got a problem with that. I don't like it."

"Maybe the real problem is that you like it too

much. At least, if the nightgown and thrills were reserved for you."

The restraint he'd managed to hang on to throughout the confrontation disintegrated before her disbelieving and perversely pleased eyes. Matthew leaned forward aggressively.

"That's right, Dee, gloat. Amuse yourself by watching me pant while you string me along. Dig those sharp little claws right in and don't stop until you're satisfied that I'm not immune to what you're flaunting. Don't you ever turn it off? It was all I could do to make it through this morning's sermon while you were zapping me from the front row—"

"I resent that." Dee shoved a finger into his chest. "You're in a fine position to talk, Mr. Holier-Than-Thou. I didn't do anything but sit there and listen while you looked at everyone but me and the kids."

"For your information, I slaved over that particular sermon for you and the kids, Ms. Jezebel." He flicked a crimson spaghetti strap. "Love the nightgown. Guess I'm lucky you didn't wear it to church this morning."

"I'm sorry I didn't," she retorted, pulling the strap back onto her shoulder. "Better luck next Sunday, huh?"

"Forget next Sunday. I want to know about tonight. Who is he? A one-night stand or a repeat coming back for more?"

"And just what or who gives you the right to ask?" She was beginning to wonder if Matthew unmasked might be more than she'd bargained for. Another little push, then she was backing off. "No, don't tell me, let me guess. You're ordained with heavenly guidance, and I'm your latest mission."

"Don't get sacrilegious with me. I don't like it, Dee. Not one damn bit." His gaze sliced her cleanly. Then he grabbed her arms and hoisted her up until she was on tiptoe and they were nose to nose. "As for you being my latest mission, lady, let me tell you, you're turning out to be the most impossible one I've taken on yet. And there've been some dandy gut wrenchers."

So she was right up there with the gut wrenchers. *Good.* It was nice to know that hers weren't the only ones getting squished. And now that she'd touched the man beneath the cloth, it was time to call a truce. He'd hurt her deeply with his earlier rejection, but she'd more than paid him back. He wasn't just hurt, he was jealous. And mad. Fighting mad. He was going to be even madder when he found out she'd set him up. Taking a deep breath, she braced herself for a backlash.

"Actually, Matthew, everything you've said tells me what I wanted to know. Now I have something to tell you. There is no other man. Not tonight. Not any night."

Several emotions chased across his face: Disbelief, surprise, relief, comprehension. And most ominous of all, fury spiked with a calculating glint in his eye.

"You're wrong," he said softly. Too softly. "There *is* a man tonight." His grip tightened on her arms and she swallowed against an uneasy foreboding. *"Me."*

"Matt—Matthew, I know you're upset and I don't blame you, but—"

"Me, upset? Noooo. Why should I be upset when you've been so thoughtful? You even selected one of my favorite pieces of music. Ravel, a perfect companion to go with the *vino.* And such stimulating conversation. I can't remember a woman ever going to such lengths to impress me. Me, upset, when you've gotten us off to a rolling good start? Certainly not. I'm ready to enjoy the fruits of your labor."

"Matthew, I—I think you should take your hands off me before you do something you might regret later."

"What's wrong?" he said smoothly. "Are they too pure for your tastes? I can remedy that." He pulled her closer, his hands relaying sensuality and tenderness that was too enticing and insistent for her to resist, even as her apprehension soared.

"Maybe you didn't hear me. I said—"

"Shut up, Dee. Hush your mouth before I do it for you." His fingers slid down her arms, and he raised her hand to his mouth and bit into the heel of her palm. Eager and sharp. Then leisurely and softly scraping. It was pleasure, exquisite pleasure.

It was also frightening, this intensity of anger and desire.

His fingertips traced a slow, burning path down her spine. His palm glided over her bottom before his fingers kneaded the flesh. She burned hot, sensitized where he touched. The sound of her response met with his low, challenging laughter.

"Eating this up, Delilah? Are you feeling a rush, some feminine sense of power by bringing the sanctimonious minister to his knees? Especially since we both know if I got on them now, it wouldn't be to say my prayers."

"You shouldn't say—be doing this." Her voice was more a languorous sigh than a protest.

"Why not? Because I'm a minister who's supposed to be more than human?"

"Yes. Yes—" Yes what? She didn't know what they were talking about anymore. All she knew was that both his hands were on her, moving over the thin silk, stroking and fondling and making it impossible for her to think.

"Don't you want to find out if a man devoted to God and humanity can lust? Aren't you just a little curious to know if you're capable of making Mr. Holier-Than-Thou lust?"

The wall must have moved, because it was suddenly behind her back and his hands were lifting her up, shifting her legs until they were wrapped around his waist. And where she was hollow and moist he was anchoring her with the ungiving bulk of his groin.

"Matt . . . Matt," she whimpered, "what . . . are you doing?"

"Lusting, that's what." He pressed into her hard with a slow, rolling grind. "I lust, Dee. *Feel me lust.*"

She lusted too. An ache gripped her, a terrible hurt that caused a moan to escape from her throat and spill past lips that were dry and in need of his.

"I feel so greedy," she whispered haltingly.

"That makes two of us, because this isn't nearly enough." His mouth found her neck and sampled it with too much leisure, nibbling and probing and lapping until she thought she might faint from the erotic treat. "You taste . . . delicious. Better than candy. Take another bite of the apple, Eve, and tell me if it's as good as the first." Then he was nipping a lobe and filling her ear with the sound of dark desire.

When she could endure no more of the tiny tortures, her head lolled against the wall, causing his teeth to rake over her skin.

"There's your sample," he said in a raspy voice as his fingertips stroked the hammering pulse in the hollow of her throat. "If you've had your fill, I'll stop."

"Stop and I'll never forgive you." Her fingers thrust into his hair, sifting through, then gripping the fine threads. Such wonderful hair, worthy of the man who held her. She pulled his head down and commanded, "Lust more, Matthew. Kiss me."

He kissed her. He kissed her as she'd never been

kissed before. Oh, the things that man did with his mouth. Their melding was more than the exchange of curious, then well-acquainted lips. More than the sly slip of an agile tongue or the nipping bites of teeth.

It was the absolute giving and giving again of exquisite pleasure filling endless need. It was the sense of devotion he brought to their kiss, the murmured words he blessed her mouth with. He said that he cared deeply. He told her this was right, wondrous, a promise he'd waited for a long time, and yes, it was worth the wait.

He said the taste of her mouth and the feel of her body was heaven.

Her body had never been in better hands. The wine had warmed her, made her reckless, but the way Matthew touched her face and back and neck created enough heat to reduce her to whimpering for more. She wasn't sure what she was saying, because she was almost incoherent with arousal, desperate for a release that was uncompromising in its demand.

"Dee," Matthew groaned. "Dee." His head fell back and she tried, without success, to press it close to her once more. "Dear Father, help me."

"*Help me,*" she pleaded. "Matthew, please, help *me.*" She was empty and crying for him to take away the ache. "I can't bear it. Don't leave me like this."

He remained still, except for taking in harsh, uneven drags of air. Then he rested his forehead against hers.

"Just be still," he whispered. "Be still with me, Delilah. We'll be all right, I promise."

"But I'm *not* all right. I've never been less right in my life."

"Shhh . . . shhhh." He laid hands on her shoulders and massaged the tense muscles. Instead of relaxing, she grew more tense, his intention to help only increasing her distress. "It's my fault. I never should have let this get out of hand. It's just that—that I needed you. I was greedy."

"And I *still* need you. Be greedy some more."

"Dee, no. I'm asking you, begging you, don't make this any more difficult for me than it is. I'm struggling, and I'm dangerously close to losing the battle."

She wanted him to lose the battle because neither of them was winning anything but martyrdom by leaving it at this.

"Is touching me, letting me touch you . . . intimately, such a terrible sin?" she demanded. "If it's so terrible, then you tell me why God made men and women the way they're made, having drives and needs that only certain people have the power to satisfy."

"Ah, Dee." His low chuckle was strained. "It's not terrible, beloved, it's beautiful and very, very special. You're special, that certain person who's made something come alive in *me*. I said I lusted and you can feel for yourself that's still true. But the problem is, I've committed myself to a standard I won't compromise. Especially with you."

He pried her legs from his waist and slid them down his length. Her belly pressed into his front and she fought not to rub against what her womb still searched for.

"All right," she said, managing a tenuous control. "I understand. Your profession stands in our way." And so much more than that. Her reasoning remained scattered, but she gathered the remains, finding enough strength not to beg him to forsake his principles and slake their desire.

"It's more than my profession," he said slowly, seeming to weigh his words. "If lust were the only thing I felt for you, I'm afraid I'd be weak enough to take what's practically killing me not to take now.

But I'm not willing to reduce what I believe we're meant to have to a moment's gratification."

The barest touch of his lips to hers was the sweetest torture. It was a humbling experience. A lesson in a kind of strength she'd never encountered in anyone but Matt. She discovered some of her own to broach an insurmountable obstacle.

"But Matthew, you don't really know me. I could be a risky deal, someone you might want more from than I can give."

"I'll take my chances. My sources upstairs tell me you're definitely a deal worth risking. They did send me to you tonight when I tried my best not to come. Then once I got here . . . out came the big guns."

"Divine intervention?"

"Mmm. Definitely divine."

"A little unconventional, don't you think?" Dee skated a fingernail down his chest. His broad, wonderful chest she craved to have for a haven . . . and if miracles came true, maybe she would one day. "Sending you over to watch me prance around half naked in my den of iniquity isn't exactly what I'd call prudent."

"The Lord moves in strange and mysterious ways." Matthew pressed her wandering hand against the heavy thudding of his heart. "I quit questioning His methods years ago." His smile was wry, intimate. "But I could question yours."

"I can hardly believe them myself." Dee laughed softly. "My only excuse is that I was feeling sorry for myself and dreaming up ways I'd like to make you fall from grace after ignoring me at lunch. I'd had a little to drink too. Actually, more than a little."

"I know. I tasted it. Very fine wine from a very naughty mouth."

"I was naughty, wasn't I?" She was slightly embarrassed but pleased. "If I'd known misbehaving could be such wicked fun, I would have tried it sooner."

"Then this sort of encounter isn't something you've . . . No, never mind. I'll trust you and not even ask."

Such a show of faith, Dee decided, deserved to be rewarded in kind. "I'll tell you anyway, Matthew. My evenings are usually spent alone in a granny gown with the lights out unless I'm curled up with a book. This was an indulgence. A very self-serving indulgence that wasn't very exciting until you showed up."

She draped her arms around his neck and he embraced her. His stubble rubbed back and forth through her hair, sending chills down to her toes.

"Yes . . . yes, exciting. Almost too exciting to stop."

"I wish it hadn't." She pulled back just far enough to see his face and take comfort that she wasn't alone in her deep sense of loss and regret.

Then Matthew shut his eyes and she felt some change in him, like a subtle shiver of energy. When he looked at her again, his expression was almost radiant, but it was shaded by an edge of conflict.

"Since I got here, I tried to keep an ear out for any sound overhead, just in case. The kids are sound sleepers?"

"Like the dead. The floors have yet to squeak at night."

He paused and stroked her hair, then asked gently, "Tell me, do you still hurt? Is the ache unbearable?"

She felt it more acutely now than she had in the throes of unsated need. The depth of connection between a man and a woman, Dee realized, could be as much of an aphrodisiac as fevered embraces.

"I do," she answered honestly. "And it is."

He nodded in empathy. "My own discomfort is my responsibility. But if you want, if your need is too much to endure, I'll take that as my responsibility too. I did create it."

She felt his palm press flat against her heat. The directness of his contact shocked her. It excited her beyond belief. Before she could recover, his hand curved in and cupped her. A broad fingertip stroked once, just once, the thin sheath of silk separating flesh from flesh.

She felt moisture between her thighs, and her legs buckled.

"Beloved," he murmured. "I can give you ease."

Seven

As Matthew gave the benediction, his narrowed gaze settled longingly on Dee's bent head. He was thankful for a lot of things that went unsaid in his concluding prayer.

He was thankful that a week earlier Dee had declined his physical offering. Her struggle to refuse what she desperately wanted to take—and he craved to give—was great. But it had reinforced his belief in her respect for others' situations and feelings. He took it as a sign that his instincts and the inner voice were right: She was the one meant for him.

He was also thankful that the homeless society he'd left to give pastorship another try had called him in for an emergency. He'd been burnt out when he left for Hayes, two hundred miles and another world away; it was good to know he had recovered and could make a difference where he continued to be needed.

He'd needed too: time and distance from Dee. Time to contemplate, search, plan. He couldn't have thought as clearly in proximity to her. She, who was tempting, mysterious, made for him.

As Maude sang the postlude, Matthew stepped

down the aisle, pausing where Dee and her family stood. At the last pew—another thing to be grateful for.

"Dee," he said in the low, confidential tone of a minister speaking a word of consolation, "I missed you."

She caught his sleeve as though by compulsion. "Yes. I missed you too." Her eyes were luminous; her face glowed as if a light shone from within. "Welcome back, Matt."

"Can you wait until everyone's gone? I'd like a word with you, alone."

Her nod was quick, hopeful, but strangely guarded.

He'd never known shaking hands to take so long. And Sally Henderson seemed to be hanging around, dusting her piano and checking for stray hymnals. He talked with Dee in an alcove about his week's work until Sally ran out of excuses to stay.

When she finally left, with a gracious parting word and a suspicious, raised brow, Matthew shook his head.

"I think she's on to us. But if she's looking for an opportunity to catch us—" He laughed and winked. "Misbehaving around here, she's flat out of luck."

Dee didn't join in his laughter. "Matthew, while you were gone I did some thinking."

"Now I'm in trouble," he jested, anticipating her retreat and ready with his argument.

"This isn't a laughing matter, Matt. You have a reputation to maintain. And I—well, I have my own life to deal with and—"

"Save your breath, Dee. My reputation is between me and the man upstairs, not anyone else. As for the other, I already know every excuse you've turned around and about in that beautiful head of yours. So you might as well give it up unless you're ready to run as fast in the opposite direction from me as you can." He detected a momentary flicker of apprehension from her, a reaction he tucked away for future reference. "Fair man that I am, I'd advise you to prepare yourself. Not only am I persistent, I can be extremely patient when the occasion demands."

Dee's gaze darted toward the church's open doors, then back to him with a longing look.

"Is that what you wanted a word alone with me for? If that's all, I'll remember your warning and go check on my roast."

"Not so fast." He caught her arm and felt the immediate surge of heat. "That roast can wait more than I can. Let's talk in my office, in case Sally remembers she forgot to water the silk flowers."

"I thought you said you were patient."

"It's never been hard for me to stay honest. I get caught in my lies every time."

Despite her obvious trepidation, Dee laughed softly, a lovely bubbling sound. He tightened his grip on her elbow and led her into the pastor's chambers. She gave a start when he shut the door behind them.

"Have a seat, Dee." He gestured to one of two chairs facing his desk, which was neat though it had its share of letters, professional magazines, and ledgers. She sat, a little nervously, he observed. All kinds of attitudes had occupied the same chair. Grief. Anger. Joy. But never had there been cause for a woman to pleat her skirt and look at him like *that*. Anxious. Desirous. Trapped and wanting to stay.

"Nice office, Matt." Her eyes lingered on his hands as he removed the long crimson sash from his shoulders. He liked that. Enough to take his time removing the robe, prolonging the simple ritual of unfastening several buttons as if he were taking off his shirt in a far more intimate setting.

"It's modest, but serves the purpose." Deciding he'd rekindled the fire of needful tension to the safest degree possible, Matt hung up the cloth, took his place behind the desk, and studied her clasped hands. "How was your week, Dee? Any luck getting some students signed up?"

"A few. The local schools put the word out, and that helped. Oh, and I wanted to thank you for welcoming us in the church bulletin. I noticed you mentioned that I had openings for piano students if anyone was interested."

"No thanks needed. I hope it helps."

"I'm surprised you got that past Mrs. Henderson. I doubt she appreciated you giving me the plug."

He shrugged. "There's no reason she should have a monopoly. Besides, her income's supplemented by the church. In the spirit of generosity, if not fair play, she should put her sour grapes aside. Tell me, has she?"

"I don't think so." The bottom of her lip disappeared between pearly teeth. *Whoa, Matthew. Later. You've got more important things to accomplish here.* "I get a distinct chill when she looks at me. I'm not going to hold my breath waiting for more flowers on my doorstep."

Whatever chill she'd encountered was distinctly absent in the room, he thought. It felt close, warm, and *ssss*, there went that finger to the iron again. He could definitely grow accustomed to having Dee close by. No flowers on her doorstep? He'd see what he could do about that.

Matthew tapped his fingers to his lips, trying to broach another concern without offending her pride. "So . . . you've signed a few students. Great! Any with promise?"

"Yes. Oh, yes, there's one." She leaned forward, nervousness replaced by animation. "He's very gifted. I understand Mrs. Henderson had reached her limit of what she could teach him, so maybe she won't mind too much that he's with me now. I've had very few students with his kind of promise, And—why are you smiling at me like that?"

"Because your eyes dance when you're excited. You have so much passion inside you—" He stopped. It was there. Right *there*. He may as well have had her against the wall with his hand between her legs and his heart pounding its way out from his ribs. Matthew took a deep breath and forced himself to focus on the matter at hand.

"What I mean is, passion for one's calling is a quality I find admirable and rare." He loosened the necktie, which had gotten tighter. "But unfortunately, it doesn't always put bread on the table. I don't know what your financial situation is, but if your practice doesn't pick up and the groceries get too slim, I'd just like you to be aware that the church sponsors a food bank and—"

"We don't need any handouts."

"I didn't mean it like that."

"Then how did you mean it?"

How? That I sense you have no one else to go to, and if you went to anyone, I'd want it to be me. That I can hide my want behind the guise of community until you learn to trust me and would willingly come to me for any need. He didn't say it. He didn't say he knew their relationship needed time to ripen; instead, he held fast to a gut-deep want and belief in providence, that the time would come. Neither did he say she was the kind of woman who would choke on her own pride before she'd let her kids do without.

"Nothing personal, Dee. I'm sorry if I offended you. It's just something I make known to newcomers in case the need ever arises. And, after working with the homeless, I guess you could say it's a matter of vocational sensitivity."

Her blush was quick, a show of embarrassment for misplaced pride and apology for elevating it above others who'd had theirs stripped. Dee's reaction only strengthened his certainty she had that special quality of empathy needed in the wife of a minister. Especially for a black sheep like him.

"Of course, Matthew. I shouldn't have snapped at you like that. You're very kind to make the offer, but we're fortunate enough not to need what other people can use. I think it's wonderful that you help the homeless. More of us should do our share and, well . . . I do have some extra time on my hands. If the food bank needs a fill-in or a delivery made, I'll be glad to lend my help."

He made a quick mental tally: *She's not too proud to apologize, but plenty proud where it counts. She's gracious. A thankful, unspoiled spirit. Willing to serve. Supportive. Yes, yes! She believes in what I do! And those breasts, oh, those luscious—*

"Consider yourself enlisted. Could your schedule handle every Tuesday from eleven to one? We have an extension of the food bank, a lunch program for shut-ins, that's in need of a delivery person."

"You don't waste any time, do you?" She laughed. Her eyes danced some more. So did his heart.

"I believe in striking while the iron's hot." Yep, kids in school. Time alone together in a car. The iron was definitely ready to strike. "By the way, you just signed onto my route. It's a two-person job. One drives, one delivers."

"Do I get to choose which position I take?"

"Take your pick, Dee. The church has a van we use for group outings and picking up some of the country kids for Sunday school. If you'd rather drive, I can deliver." Of course he'd happily oblige her both ways once he got a commitment from her. "We can even trade, if you'd like." Yes sir, he was an equal opportunity lover in his heart.

"Sounds like a deal." They shared a gaze that deliciously lengthened until Dee reached for her purse. "I guess I should go. The kids have probably let the roast burn by now. Was there anything else you wanted to mention?"

"Yes. What happened last week." His reply was swift. So was the drop of Dee's purse and her quick intake of breath. He'd caught her off guard, as intended. As for secret pasts and future commitments, they would discuss those in good time. "I've thought about it a lot. What about you?"

"Some," she hedged. "I've had other things going on. You know, homework, interviewing potential students and—I'm sorry, Matt, last Sunday hasn't been at the top of my list."

Matthew remained calm while Dee nervously worked a sexy high heel up and down the back of her foot. The longer he contemplated her, the faster she worked it. Once the movement was close to a shimmy, he pounced.

"I get the feeling you've thought about what we shared more than a little, but it's something you're afraid to discuss. What are you scared of?"

"There's nothing to discuss. We argued. We acted on impulse. I was drunk—"

"Look, Dee, I've seen enough drunks, and unfortunately I've been sloshed enough times myself, to know the difference between don't-know-what-I'm-doing irrational behavior and I'm-feelin'-good-and-doing-exactly-what-I-want honest responses. You knew exactly what you were doing, saying, feeling. And I certainly did. It happened. It's not going away, no matter how much either of us could try to pretend otherwise. We have to talk about this. I want to talk about it now."

Dee shut her eyes. She should have known better than to come to church today. That was no different from waving a red flag in front of a bull. But she'd been desperate to see him, even if from the back pew. *Had she thought about that incredible night?* A night when she'd come alive beneath this man's giving touch, had learned what it meant to be a woman, to be cherished and to discover a dormant chord she hadn't realized existed until Matt brought it to life.

Had she thought of anything else? Only that she missed him terribly and wanted him in a way that could never be.

"You're right, Matthew. It did happen. I enjoyed it. But pleasure has a price, and a repetition of last week's indulgence could be more than either of us can really afford. As I said, you have a reputation to maintain. From the comments Loren and Jason are bringing home from school, mine's not too great. I like you . . . tremendously. And yes, I'm more than a little attracted. But you're a good man and those are in short supply. And I know you're smart enough to enjoy a minor indiscretion and then leave well enough alone."

"Well, well," he said, seemingly to himself. "And she's sacrificial too. You sure know how to pick 'em." Matthew leaned back in his chair, looking very self-satisfied for a man who'd been given the brush-off. He was smiling as if he'd put a flag on Mt. Everest instead of tumbling down and being buried under a heap of snow.

"Then you agree we should put last week behind us and go on as friends?" she said, deflated at the prospect.

He tapped a finger to his mouth. She wished he'd quit that. She didn't need any reminders of just how adroit his mouth was. What she needed was him. She needed him without all the garbage defining her life. She needed him because of all the garbage defining her life. He had to back off for both their sakes. If he backed off, she'd die.

And if Matt got too involved with her, they both could.

"Not exactly," he finally said. "Has anyone, by chance, ever told you what an incredible kisser you are?"

Had anyone told *him*?

"Matthew! You need to listen to me. This is important."

"Okay, you're right, this is important. We need to agree on a solution. Any suggestions?"

Suggestions? Could she have an affair with a small-town minister when staying invisible was mandatory? Right. That would be as sane as jumping over Niagara Falls. She could get the hell out of Hayes before she made Loren's curtains. *Really mature and nurturing, Dee,* she scolded herself. Just when her dependents had a semblance of home and stability she could uproot them again because of her own weaknesses. Just when she'd met the true meaning of strength, she could run for cover and never forget him.

For some reason, Dee had the strangest feeling Matthew would hunt her down. Then she'd have Vince, Nick, *and* Matthew hot on her trail. If they all got together, Armageddon could commence right there.

Dee was tired of running. She was loathe to subject Jason and Loren to any more trauma than they'd already endured. And her own needs, so long shelved, were demanding attention.

"We could be friends," she ventured to say while the internal dispute raged. "I'd like to be friends."

"I'm counting on it. Anything else?"

"You could fix my leaky faucets if you're free and feeling generous with your time."

"Faucets, no problem. What about picnics?"

"Picnics?"

"Say, next Saturday. I'll bring the wine and

bread if you'll bring thou and the kids. Be sure to tell Jason not to forget his football."

"So you're agreed to friendship and picnics with little hellions?"

"Give me two months. A kiss says those little hellions may never be angels, but I can influence the amount of fire and brimstone flung between them while you're caught in the middle. *If* you'll share the reins when I'm around."

"Since when did kisses enter the picture?"

"Since I can't quit thinking about them every time you're on my mind. Which is close to constant."

Dee fumbled for her handbag. Memories of what they'd shared and the impossibility of more collided.

"I'd better go." She wasn't certain she'd stood and reached the door until Matthew's hand flattened against it, barring her escape. "Let me out, Matt. It's past time I left."

"I disagree." His free hand clamped around her wrist and stroked the soft pulse point. Frantic, she jiggled the knob, then gave up. Running was futile. Unlike Vince, who controlled by power and favors owed, Matthew asserted another kind of authority. An invisible power that made Vince's quell in comparison. "We're not finished with our negotiations, Dee. Did I forget to mention I can drive a hard bargain?"

"Please, Matt, dinner is probably burning."

"Let it." Pulling her hand from the knob, he pressed his lips into her palm. "We can be friends, but I want more. How do you feel about kisses? *My* kisses."

"This isn't the time or place for that kind of discussion. Someone—Mrs. Henderson could come in."

He locked the door, silently assuring her that wouldn't happen.

"I want kisses included in the deal."

"What kind of kissing?" she asked quickly.

"All kinds. Nice kisses. Good-night kisses. Soft ones, deep ones. And in case you didn't notice, I like to French. Wet and hot, but not too messy."

The man was dangerous. If he didn't let her out now, she would surely succumb to his sensual persuasion. He'd exchanged his hand-kissing for a slow exploration of her temple. She felt the flick of his tongue before he moved to the front of her forehead.

"Just kisses, nothing else?"

"I'll stick with kisses until we're ready for more."

"Then what happened last week—"

"Won't happen again. Not for a while anyway. We'll take it slow. Okay?"

"If I agree, will you let me go?"

"Anxious, Dee?" His thumb stroked over her throat before settling against the pounding hollow. "Good thing my self-esteem's in decent working order. A man could get his ego bruised if he thought a woman agreed to let him kiss her just to get away."

"All right, then, you can have kisses. Friends and picnics and—and kisses. That's it. Kisses and . . . the roast is burning."

His chuckle was intimate. So was the way he turned her in his arms and looked at her with a mixture of desire and affection and something else she couldn't define.

"You're not living up to your bad reputation. Something tells me certain people would be disappointed. I'm not." His fingertip crooked under her chin and raised her face. "You can go. Just one minor detail needs taking care of first." His head lowered. "Sealing our bargain with . . . a . . . *kiss*."

She was lost. At the first touch of his lips to hers, she was lost. Her arms went around his neck and he gathered her to him. His chest was heavy against her breasts, his hands roved gently against her back. And his belt buckle was pressed against her. She felt the whole of him as she absorbed all he had to give.

Her mouth didn't need coaxing to open and his made no apology for getting down to business. His tongue was fleet and sure; her own had trouble keeping up with his clever mastery of her mouth. When he took his tongue back, she murmured a protest.

"Sorry, but that's all for today." He kissed her forehead once, then unlocked the door. "You'd better go check on that roast before it burns."

To hell with the roast. *She* burned. "What do you mean, that's all for today?"

"Guess I forgot to mention one last, crucial detail." He smiled a very smug, unministerlike smile. "Just to make sure what happened last week doesn't happen again until it should, we're relegated to only one kiss per meeting. You might keep that in mind, since next time's your turn."

"One kiss! My turn!" Was the man insane? Sadistic? He had to be kidding, surely. "Are you playing with me?"

"Don't I wish." The way he looked her over left no doubt about that. "Unfortunately, those are the rules. Enjoy your dinner and I'll see you Tuesday. Eleven sharp."

"I don't suppose meal deliveries count as meetings," she quipped, sufficiently thwarted to be peevish.

"Hmmm . . . let me think about that. In the meantime, you give some thought to kissing me back."

"You mean—"

"I went first so you'd get an idea of what kind of kissing I'd like in return."

"Are you sure there aren't some time limitations you failed to mention too?"

Matthew's brow furrowed as if he were pondering world peace. "Hadn't thought about that. But it's probably a good idea. How does five minutes max hit you?"

"Ten," she countered.

"Seven and a half."

"Deal."

The roast did burn. As Dee scraped the meat from the pan, she found herself humming.

She stopped.

She was happy, she realized. The roast she couldn't afford was burned and she was walking on air. Happiness wasn't a state she'd been familiar with for a good while. It felt wonderful, sublime. Addictive.

And, therefore, dangerous. A trap she could easily fall into and be incapable of giving up. But she needed happiness. She deserved at least a little, didn't she? She'd lost so much. Everything she'd ever loved or worked for gone, except for Jason and Loren.

For them, if not for her, she had to be careful. Yet what could a little happiness hurt? She couldn't let herself fall in love. She couldn't even consider a commitment.

But picnics were okay.

And so were seven-and-a-half-minute kisses.

Eight

Dee pounded a fist into her pillow for the umpteenth time. She tossed. She turned. She gave up and flicked on her bedside lamp.

She groaned aloud. "I should have taken it while the taking was good. Him and his kisses. Two months of swapping spit, and I'm ready to scream."

Dee sighed wearily. Then she smiled and impulsively hugged herself tight, pretending it was Matthew's arms holding her in the aloneness of her bed. Well, she told herself, at least he'd increased the time limit. And, except for the one week per month he left town to work with the homeless, their meetings were frequent.

Picnics. Sunday drives. Tuesday meal deliveries to shut-ins. They even attended PTA meetings together. Matthew was everything his adopted family had never had. He was unstinting support and a barrel of laughs. He was hell behind the pulpit yet he never pounded, only speaking wisely and with conviction.

He was a damn good kisser. And an incredible lover. That is, when she could forget her frustrations long enough to fall asleep and make love with him in her dreams.

She heard a squeaking overhead, the same sound her bed made in her dreams.

A minute later Loren tapped at her open door. "Dee? Can I come in?"

"Sure, princess." Dee glanced at her bedside clock while Loren perched on the mattress's end and tucked up her legs. "It's eleven o'clock. Did you have another bad dream?"

"I haven't gone to sleep yet. There's something I wanted to ask you about but I kind of hate to."

"You can talk to me." Talking with Loren had become vastly easier of late. Matt had asked for a hand with the kids, and he'd gotten it. Firm but fair, he had a special gift for enforcing discipline and commanding respect. They were all reaping the benefits of his influence—an influence that had him taking some heat from his congregation, she was sure, though he avoided the topic.

"What's wrong, Loren? Has someone been harassing you again at school about your 'bad mama screwing the what-a-babe preacher'?"

Dee repeated the remarks Loren had come home with since Matt's courtship had ensued without apology and openly enough for anyone with eyes to see. Jason had borne the brunt too, sporting more than one black eye for defending his "parents." The black eyes hadn't been very frequent since Matt had given him lessons in verbal defense, followed by a more direct approach—avoiding an on-target slug with a slide of the foot behind an opponent's. And if that didn't work, a stomach punch ended things quick.

"It's not that," Loren said. "It's about a Christmas program the junior high's having. I want to go to the party after the play, but it's pretty fancy. I mean, the girls in my class are talking about what to wear. They all want to get dressed up in prom stuff, and I don't have anything like that. I know we don't have tons of money, Dee."

Dee's heart contracted. She herself hadn't grown up rich, but an appropriate dress had never been too much to ask for. Loren *had* grown up rich, and now she was worried about dollars and cents. With good cause. Dee's modest savings were being depleted by the day, and even with her increasing enrollment of piano students, there wasn't enough money to make ends meet. In less than half a year they could be asking for the food bank's help she'd refused unless things picked up or she got a part-time job.

But that was *her* problem, not those of a teenager who deserved the joy of being young before she became an adult.

"We can swing it, Loren. Two new students start this week and we're getting by fine." She squeezed Loren's hand. "Now, quit worrying about it. We'll take a long drive soon and get you something really cool from Des Moines. It'll be fun, just us girls."

"I'd really like that."

"Me too. I'm proud of you, Loren. Your grades are good and no detentions."

"Mama's proud," Loren said quietly.

"Yes, your mama is proud of you, princess—" A sudden light tapping against the window caused them both to stiffen.

"Dee—"

"Shhh." Her heart pounding, she turned off the light and got out of bed, slowly inching toward the window.

"Maybe we should call Matthew."

"No," Dee whispered sharply. "Just be quiet." The drapes trembled in her grasp. Should she peek from the side or use the element of surprise and jerk them open? She should have gotten the gun she'd bought and hidden beneath the mattress. Without it, covertness was her best choice.

She peered outside. "It's okay," she said with a rush of relief. Dee stared at the branch tapping against the glass. "It's just a tree. You can relax."

The fear that had filled up the room was replaced by the palpable resentment emanating from the girl huddled beneath the covers.

"I hate Vince. I really hate him, Dee. He's not even here and he's still scaring us."

"And that's exactly why we have to be careful about everything we say or do. Not even Matthew can know, understand? If you're ever alone and something like this happens and you can't find me, then call him. But whatever you do, don't tell him about Vince."

"Or Nick? He's as bad as Vince, even if he is a lawyer and my uncle."

"How do you know?" Dee turned on the lamp, wanting the security of light and a better look at Loren's face. "I never talked to you about my relationship with him."

"Aw, c'mon. I might've been young, but I saw you kissing him and him trying to feel you up when you thought I wasn't looking. And he was around the house so much. Major barf." A mischievous smile sparked her lips. "Bet he wasn't as good a kisser as Matthew."

"Young lady, my love life isn't any of your business." Despite her resolve to be firm, Dee couldn't suppress a girlish giggle. "But you're right. Matthew's the best kisser. The best everything."

"Are you in love with him?"

Was she? Could a woman be in love and still keep so many invisible walls between herself and the man she craved to bond with completely?

"I do love Matthew."

"Well, of course you love him. Everyone loves Matthew. Even me and Jason. What I mean is—"

"I know what you mean." The phone on the

nightstand rang. Dee glanced at the clock. Eleven twenty-two. A call this late was odd. "Saved by the bell," she said, trying to hide her apprehension before she answered cautiously, "Hello?"

"Did I wake you up?"

"Matt, it's you." Her heart immediately flip-flopped at the sound of his vibrant, rich voice.

"It'd better be me." He chuckled. "You know how I get when I'm jealous. Not a pretty sight."

"I miss you," she confessed.

"I miss you too. I haven't seen you for three whole hours." The sound of a soft kiss relayed itself over the wires.

"You already had your allotment of that for the day," she teased, winding her finger around the cord.

"Wanna dock me on the next one?"

"No! We'll let this time slide. Be partners in crime—" Her smile faded. "Is that why you called?"

"To steal a kiss? Not a bad idea. But the real reason is that . . . I had the feeling something wasn't quite right. I wanted to make sure you were okay."

He never ceased to amaze her. His attunement to her every emotion and thought was like a direct pipeline that flowed between them, as if the damn-able barriers didn't exist.

"I'm fine, Matthew." In a whisper she added, "You make me fine."

"Wish I could make it with you," he murmured silkily.

"Matthew! What a thing for a minister to say."

"What did he say?" Loren eagerly asked.

"I heard that." Matthew laughed. "Tell her I said it's past her bedtime and if she doesn't hit the sack I won't introduce her to that so-fine nephew of mine next week."

"Are you really sure taking us to your parents'

house for Thanksgiving is a good idea?" Dee's stomach rolled over at the thought. "Your whole family's going to be there, and I'm afraid we'll be in the way."

"My whole family won't be there unless you and the kids come along. You know how I feel about you guys." His pause lengthened while Dee felt a warmth radiate and spread through her. "Besides, I really need you with me. I haven't seen my folks for a few years, and this is a visit I'm not relishing. It could be strained. If you don't want to deal with that over the holidays, I can make the trip another time. Either way, I want us to spend Thanksgiving together."

"Then we'll come along. Besides, Loren would never forgive me for putting the skids on her meeting your nephew." Their combined sound of humor was forced. "Matthew," she continued, "do you want to talk about them? Your parents."

"No, Dee. Some other time. It's a long story and one I don't want to get into tonight."

Or any other night, it seemed. He'd let her know there was a long-standing rift between him and his father, but more than that he wouldn't say. She wanted to probe, to be his listening ear and side-taker. But who was she to dig into his past when she covered her own like a grave?

"Okay, Matt. But if you change your mind—"

"I know." A significant silence. "And so do you."

"Good night, Matthew. Sweet dreams."

"If they're about you, they will be."

Dee stared at the cradled receiver while the bedside clock ticked off thought-filled seconds.

"Can I sleep with you tonight, Dee? I'm still a little shook up from our scare."

"Sure." Summoning a smile, she turned off the light. "I could use a snuggling partner too, princess."

In the dark she heard Loren's small whisper. "Good night, Mama. I love you."

Dee found her hand beneath the covers and squeezed it. Then said a silent prayer for Matthew and Loren and Loren's mama.

"It's my turn to play Game Boy." Jason snatched the hand-held Nintendo from his sister. They were on the backseat of the church van, which was sailing down the interstate.

"Give that back! I'm not through with my game yet and—You screwed up my score. Now I get my turn all over again."

"Straighten up," Matthew shouted over the ruckus. With his left hand on the steering wheel, he released Dee's shoulder and reached back with his right. "Hand it over, Jason. Loren, I'd better not hear you talking like that again, do you understand?"

"Hand it over?" they protested jointly.

"But I'm bored," Jason said.

"Yeah," Loren seconded. "Jeez, how much longer do we have to—"

"The Game Boy, Jason?"

"Dee, you're not gonna let him take it, are you?"

"He's acting like he thinks he's our father. He's not our father—"

"That's enough out of you, Loren." Dee shot her a censuring glare. She'd never seen Matthew so ill tempered with the kids, his wick seeming to shorten with each mile they got closer to his parents' home. Her own nerves were shot, her uneasiness over meeting them turning to dread.

Matthew snapped his fingers, demanding the Game Boy. Jason and Loren stared at Dee, silently demanding she take their side. If this was any indication of what the rest of their holiday would be like, she was ready to make a demand of her own and insist they turn the van around.

"Dee?" Matthew expected her to back him up, she knew. She thought he was being a little unreasonable, but that wasn't the real issue.

"Give him the Game Boy, Jason."

"But—"

"You heard your mother." Matt claimed the battle prize and plopped it in Dee's lap. "Thanks," he said under his breath.

"Really, Matt," she whispered. "Was that necessary? We've got over a hundred miles to go."

"Bear with me, Dee." His glance was troubled. "Please?"

She squeezed his knee. "Just try to remember we'll have this behind us in a few days."

"I hope. There is a chance we'll leave sooner, so be prepared."

"I'll have another talk with the kids about using their best manners."

"They're not the ones I'm worried about." He grasped her hand, and she realized his was clammy.

"Are you sure you want to go through with this?"

"No, I'm not. But this visit's past due. If it gets too awkward, we can always cut out early."

"I wish you would tell me what's going on. All I know is that your dad's a minister and the two of you had a falling out when you decided to serve in a less conservative church. That doesn't seem like much of a reason for him to be upset with you."

"It goes a bit further than that. Keep your ears open, and I'm sure you'll get the gist of his gripe."

"I'd rather hear the whole story from you."

"Later, Dee. For now it's nothing that affects you."

"Well, it affects *you* and because of that it does

affect me." The glance he shot her let Dee know he could say the same thing. He said nothing though; none of them did.

Twenty miles down the road, Matt broke the silence.

"Make you a deal, kids. You can have the Game Boy back as long as you promise not to squabble. Fair enough?"

"Yeah."

"Sure."

"Okay, but who gets it first?" Matthew asked.

"I do," Jason said.

"Loren, what say you?"

"I say . . . give it to Jason."

"But you didn't get to finish your game before I took it away."

"That's okay. It's not worth fighting about or getting it taken away again because we can't agree."

"In that case . . ." Matthew winked at Dee as he scooped up the item in dispute. Handing it over the seat, he said, "You get it first, Loren."

"I do?"

"Not fair," Jason said with a huff.

"It's very fair." Matthew pulled Dee close to his side. "You were selfish. Loren wasn't. She deserves first rights, and that's my final decision. If you want to argue with my authority, I can arrange for her to have it the rest of the trip. Any questions?"

"No, sir."

When Dee looked approvingly over the seat, she was no less than amazed to see Loren slip the Game Boy to Jason and put a finger to her lips.

The old saying about mothers having eyes in the back of their heads apparently extended to self-appointed fathers. Dee saw a satisfied smile curve Matt's lips.

"If I didn't know better," she said softly, "I'd think I was sitting next to King Solomon himself."

"I'm afraid not, Dee." His smile thinned to a straight, grim line. "You're coming home with the prodigal son."

Nine

"Matthew, would you please say grace?"

"My pleasure, Dad." While twenty heads bowed, Matthew reached beneath the table and grasped Dee's hand. She squeezed it tight. Bless her. One night and half a day at his parents' home had drained him dry and left his throat raw from choking back quick retorts to his father's subtle reminders that their impasse had far from disappeared.

"Lord, with glad hearts we gather together to celebrate this special day of Thanksgiving with You and each other. We do appreciate this feast, which is generous. Bless those who aren't as lucky as ourselves and even as You forgive us our shortcomings, help us to forgive one another. In a word, thanks a lot, can't wait to dig in. Amen."

"Amen" was echoed all around. With a single exception.

"'Thanks a lot, can't wait to dig in?'" Carlton Peters repeated tersely in a low voice. Presiding at the head of the long table and seated beside Matthew, he looked reprovingly over wire-rimmed glasses at his son. "Is that how you pray at your church? Talking to God like a pal instead of with the show of respect you were raised to do?"

Matthew slapped some mashed potatoes onto his mother's best china with more force than was needed to clear the spoon.

"Potatoes, Dad?" Matt was thankful that his brother and three sisters and their kids were talking with Dee, Loren, and Jason while his mother ran to the kitchen to take the rolls out of the oven before they burned. If anything was burning, it was Matt.

"I just lost my appetite." The elder Reverend Peters, head pastor of a thousand-member church, handed the proferred dish to his daughter. "You might have put the robes back on, but you haven't really changed, have you, Matthew?"

"Can we discuss this later? Mom's worked hard and it is Thanksgiving. I have guests and I'd really appreciate your saving this for another time."

"You show up after we haven't seen you for years and you expect me to hold my tongue?" His voice remained subdued but sharp. "Last time you brought a bunch of hoods on Harleys. This go-around you bring a divorced woman with two kids to our table, along with the insinuation that this is the first Thanksgiving of many you'd like to spend with them. You know well and good my views on divorce and marriage. Tell me, Matthew, are you deliberately trying to hurt and shame me more than you already have, or are you perpetually stupid?"

Matthew stopped carving the turkey. His jaw worked back and forth. He, too, kept his voice low so no one else would hear, though the urge to shout was immense.

"You can attack me and my principles all you like. But don't ever, *ever* speak in that snide tone about the woman beside me again. Marriage is sacred to me, and I've waited a long time for the right woman to come into my life. Belittle my judgment if you must, but God help you if I detect so much as a whisper of criticism directed at her."

"If He needs to help anyone, it's *you*."

Seeing his mother return, Matthew took the old familiar admonishment with the stamina of a retired fighter climbing back into the ring. With effort, he retreated to rethink his strategy and save up his strength.

"Chill out, Dad. This can wait until we're alone. It's not right for us to spoil everyone else's dinner."

"Their dinner, my reputation and life." Carlton's fist landed on the table. Eighteen heads turned at the force of his strike. "When, just tell me when, Matthew, are you going to quit thinking about yourself and act responsibly, with some kind of discretion for once?"

"And you're being discreet? I wish you could listen to yourself, Dad. And as for me thinking of no one but myself, what about you? Where is *your* forgiveness and compassion? Maybe discretion isn't my strong suit, but at least I see the world and the people in it through eyes that aren't as narrow as a needle's. Everything's so black and white for you that you can't appreciate the beauty of life's colors. You haven't changed. And barring a miracle, I doubt you ever will."

"Heaven knows it would take more than a miracle to straighten you out, Matthew. We raised you with love and a sense of right and wrong—"

"Not everything's right or wrong, Dad. For once in your life can't you open your eyes and see? If you had your way, Adam would have been castrated in Eden and the world ended before it had a chance to start."

"Blasphemy! Blasphemy is what you speak. You shame me. For years you've shamed me. Leave this table and don't come back unless you can apologize to me with more than words. Your thinking is wrong, and until you can right it we have nothing left to say."

"At least we agree on one thing." Matthew threw down his napkin. "As far as I'm concerned, this Thanksgiving is over. And so are we." He got up so fast, his chair hit the wall behind him. Matt shifted his gaze to his mother, who covered her mouth as tears filled her eyes. "I'm sorry, Mom. I tried, so help me, I did. I thought it could work this time, but I have to admit that my thinking was grossly wrong. Dee. Jason and Loren. I hate to cut dinner short, but it's time we left."

The rest of the family had put down forks and knives and were mute. His mother was now openly crying, saying that she loved him, then pleading with Carlton to stop this horrible thing and give them all some peace.

Clearly stunned, Dee just stared at Matthew. He reached for her arm and pulled her up. The way she and the children followed him meekly to the door told Matthew two things: They supported him without question. And they weren't novices in the witnessing of heated disputes.

They made the trip back to Hayes in silence. Dee sat close to Matthew's side and held his hand.

By the time they pulled up to her cottage, Jason and Loren were nodding off. They promptly went upstairs to bed.

"Matthew, would you like a glass of wine?"

"I'd prefer scotch, if you've got it. A double on the rocks."

He was staring grimly ahead when a glass appeared under his nose. "Thanks," he said shortly. "Do me a favor and turn off the lights."

Seconds later the room was covered in darkness. Then he heard the strike of a match and saw a candle flame leap. He felt her sit beside him as a soothing new age instrumental trickled into the silence.

"You've had some experience with ugliness, haven't you?" he asked.

"More than I'd like," was her soft reply.

"Sorry to add more to it, Dee. I had thought time would ease the animosity. If I'd known otherwise, I never would have pulled you and the kids into it. We could have stayed here and shared Thanksgiving the way it was meant to be enjoyed. My oversight. Or maybe my ongoing refusal to bend."

"Matthew. My Matthew." She made his name a much-needed caress. The touch of her hand on his was even more needed. "Drink your scotch. Kiss me. Talk to me. Whatever helps, whatever I can do, just tell me. You're hurting. I hurt for you. And I hurt even more to think I contributed to what happened today."

"Believe me, had I gone alone, it would have ended the same. Worse, since you wouldn't have been there to share in my mess." The liquor burned down his throat.

"How bad is the mess, Matthew?"

"You saw for yourself. One helluva mud-slinging mess." He polished off the last drop, taking no time to savor the liquor. He hadn't indulged in serious imbibing since he'd hung up his leather jacket. Dee's quick refill of his glass struck him as the action of a woman accustomed to catering to worldly men. He didn't like that. It also told him nothing he could say would shock her. And for that he was glad, since it was time he came clean.

"Look, Dee, it's like this. I was expelled from my first pastorship. Less than two years, and boom came the drop-kick. I'd tried to conform, but little differences of opinion became big ones. I ended up stepping on a lot of toes. They branded me a heretic for speaking what I thought truthful and blackballed me from future service in the denomination I was raised in. A denomination where my father is very high-profile. I'm not saying their philosophy is wrong, but I felt I had the right to express my beliefs. Unfortunately, mine didn't mesh with theirs."

"How terrible for you, Matt."

"Yeah, it was. But even worse was Dad turning his back on me to join with the side his bread was buttered on. He said he did what his conviction told him to do. I held to the fact that he'd taught me to do the same, but unlike him and his peers, the only thing I was intolerant of was intolerance." He snorted derisively. "Funny, I hadn't realized until then the man I grew up almost idolizing had such a double standard. He could tolerate anyone or anything but his son's fall from grace."

Matt's laugh was bitter and short. "And let me tell you, did I fall then. It became my personal mission in life to raise holy hell."

Dee's reaction was to sift her fingertips through his hair and press a tender kiss to his neck.

"Were you bad?" A smile was almost in her voice.

"Honey, let me tell you, I was the baddest of the bad. At least I tried my best to be. Sold every possession I owned to stay afloat, even my car. I bought a motorcycle and took off. Halfway across the country I hooked up with a biker gang."

"You?" Her smile became outright laughter. "Matthew, that's wild!"

"It was wild, all right." He chuckled himself, glad for some black humor. "Midnight rides, tough women, brawls in bars. Only I had this problem. Every time a fight started, I automatically took the role of peacemaker. Whenever anyone got beaten up or threw up from too much of a good time, guess who tended them? And there was always someone with a personal difficulty or emotional conflict. Word got around that the dude into meditating wasn't bad in the advice department. Just couldn't help myself."

"So you helped whoever needed helping."

"Something like that. So much for my attempt at being one mean, macho man. I rode with them for a couple of years, then one day we cruised into a city where I saw a woman on a corner holding a little baby and a sign. The sign read HOMELESS. WILL WORK FOR FOOD. HELP ME FEED MY BABY. Made me want to cry. Still does, just thinking about it."

"Me too." Dee's eyes were moist. He loved her eyes. He loved *her*. In Dee's eyes he could more than forget the shadow of his past, the distance from his father. He could possibly begin to forgive.

Something inside him softened, something that had been wounded and hardened. With no more than her gaze, her alignment with his position, he felt himself begin the slow journey to mending. It was a wondrous thing. The beauty of it humbled him.

"Well, Dee, before I knew it, I'd passed the hat, or, rather, bandanna around and everyone pitched in to make sure the woman and her baby had enough to eat for a week. I remember thinking, What am I doing burning rubber when other people don't even have food? How selfish, how irresponsible. I felt I was much worse than my ex-church had made me out to be. So I quit fighting God and myself, said so long to my pals, and found the nearest homeless organization. The same one I work with now."

"But you left."

"It was time. Six years there took its toll. A person can see only so much poverty and hopelessness before he starts hardening himself to what's around him. Especially when he's alone. And I was. No one to share my fatigue with, or my anger for not being able to make more of a difference." Her cheek was soft beneath his stroking fingertip. If he'd had this, had Dee, maybe he could have stayed with it and made more of a difference. "I *was* alone," he said quietly. "But then came you."

She leaned into his touch. She looked as if she were about to say something important, to return his need for more of a commitment. But then she shook her head and pulled back slightly. Her following words weren't what Matthew wanted, needed, to hear.

"Do you ever see your biker friends?"

"We keep in touch. They know where I am even if I don't know what road trip they're on. I'm sure you'll meet them since they're planning a visit this spring." He shook with quiet laughter. "That should be quite a scene when they come roaring into Hayes, but I'll be damned before I ever turn my back on a friend or exclude any soul from God's house."

"Then the church doesn't know about you riding with them?"

"Hell, no! I'm not as perpetually stupid as my father thinks I am. I wanted this job. Needed it. It was the chance to prove I could make the cut as a pastor. In a far more tolerant church, mind you. Someone gave me the lead at the homeless office and I went for it." He paused, courting back the lost intimacy. "Thank goodness, since we wouldn't have met. Divine providence, Dee. I believe it. I hope you believe it too." He touched her lips and whispered, "Beloved."

Again he felt that moment of bonding. Again it eluded his grasp.

"Does the church know about you getting ousted before?"

"Let's say that my ex-affiliation wasn't nearly as interesting to this church as my credentials from college and seminary. I had a good track record with the homeless organization, and they were concerned with promoting community awareness of the needy. The scandal had died by the time these good people met me, and I didn't bring it up. My tracks should be covered, unless you decide to squeal on me."

"Matthew, you never cease to amaze me. *You*, a member of a biker gang, pastoring a church in Hayes." Dee chortled. "Talk about divine providence. That we met here . . . is incredible."

"As incredible as my being any kind of real biker. Actually I was more of an honorary member. Kind of a mascot. I understand they still laugh about the time I passed out when a tattoo artist pulled out his needles and went to work."

"You have a tattoo?" she said excitedly. "Where? Can I see it?" Her eyes lit up at the prospect.

"Why do I have the feeling you're getting a kick out of my less than successful attempt to live sordidly?"

"Please, Matthew?"

He raised a brow and smiled wickedly. "I have two. Considering where they're located, you might want to, ah, contemplate that request. Just don't contemplate too hard."

"You mean they're located in . . . private places?"

"One is. The other's not so private, but I'd have to take off some clothing for you to see. Interested, Dee? I don't know about you, but kisses and only kisses are taxing my patience." Her swallow was visible. He delighted in having that effect on her. Was it possible that he could use the intensity of their attraction to get that commitment he desired even more than her sweet, luscious body?

Dee had grown accustomed to Matthew's small silences and moments of absolute stillness. But this was different. His face was shaded by an intensity she recognized: Purpose.

To what end, she wasn't sure. Then he led her hands to his chest, and she knew. His purpose was *passion*.

Kisses and sweet caresses were one thing, but this irreversible turn in their relationship could make every wall she loathed, but was frantic to keep, come tumbling down. Dee quickly took her hands back and started talking fast.

"Maybe you can show me the tattoo later. Now tell me what sort of differences of opinion caused your first church to evict you. You seem pretty traditional to me . . . in an unconventional way, that is."

As he leaned back he let out a stream of air through his teeth that sounded like a hiss of frustration. Then he stretched his arms on the couch's worn back. The motion caused his shirt to tighten against his chest and shoulders, the cuff to rise up his wrist, revealing a bit of dark masculine hair. Did his chest have hair? Dee wondered. If so, how much and what would be the texture? Coarse and thick or perhaps soft and sworled in a seductive pattern? Would it flow short of his navel, or dip beneath? Her face grew warm, and she feared she was too openly expressing her own want and frustration.

When she returned her attention to his face, she saw a sly smile touched his lips.

"So you'd like to know what differences of opinion set me apart?" He unbuttoned his top button, then stretched again. "There were quite a few, but the one that comes to mind at the moment has to do with my views on premarital sex. When I counseled unmarried couples it ummm . . . came up a few times."

Had she knocked down Pandora's box and scattered its contents in her mad rush to shut the lid? Dee swallowed hard.

"You don't believe in it, right?" she said quickly.

"Quite the contrary," he replied smoothly. "I do. What about you?"

"I—well, I think it depends on the people involved."

"You mean whether they love each other or if it's just a shallow exchange of body parts?"

"Ah . . . yes."

"I couldn't agree more."

"You actually told young people it was okay to go all the way as long as they loved each other?"

"Not quite." He caught her hand, which she'd pressed at her throat, and kissed her palm before urging it to his chest. His heart beat heavily; hers was closer to a drum roll. "It was and *is* my opinion that two mature, consenting adults who have a verbal commitment—as in 'I love you, need you, and want to spend the rest of my life with you'—don't need legal papers to sanctify a physical union that heaven respects."

Dee rubbed the button beneath her finger, torn between releasing it and rushing Matthew out the door.

"I love you, Dee." His simple statement jolted her. "I also need you and respect you. If you can return those feelings, I have faith that the rest will work itself out. My belief in our future would be strong enough for me to take you to bed tonight. Say that you love me," he softly commanded.

The sweetest, most intoxicating rush flowed through her veins. No man had ever said he loved her like that. No man had ever looked at her with such honesty and complexity of emotion: Love, in all its glory. Selfless. Devoted. Needy. *Sexual.*

But Matthew's purpose exceeded passion. He was after a deeper commitment she'd give her soul to make. And once given, she wouldn't be able to disguise the truth.

"I'm not ready to say that, Matthew." The words cut into her heart. "And besides, you've been through a lot today. What you're wanting from me could be only a reaction to your needing my support and me giving it—gladly. Let that be enough. We shouldn't say or do anything you might regret tomorrow once the hurt and anger start to wear off."

"The only thing that hurts and angers me is your rejection when I'm telling you in no uncertain terms that I need more from our relationship than friendship and kisses."

The pointed flick of his thumb over her white satin blouse caused her nipple to bead. She inhaled sharply.

"Matthew, please." Her voice was urgent. "We have to stop this. *Now*."

His fingertips folded sternly about her jaw, and he studied her long and incisively.

"Has a man abused you before? Is that why you're refusing to give us what we need? I know the real reason is that you're scared of something. Don't lie to me, Dee. I'll be able to tell if you do."

"No, Matt. I swear to you. I haven't been physically mistreated. Not the way you're thinking."

"But what, then? I want to know why you're afraid of intimacy when you're as hungry for it as I am. Why you won't return my love when I can feel it so strongly inside you. Something's dogging you, and I want to know what it is."

"I need more time," she said frantically. "More time, that's all."

"I've given you time. We know each other better, feel more for each other than most of the couples I've counseled. And we're talking people who've been married for years." He rubbed a hand over his forehead.

"Ah, hell . . . " He snorted in disgust. "I say we know each other, but that's not exactly true. Tonight I told you what I wouldn't speak to another soul. And still you keep this thing between us. Don't you ever get sick of it, Dee? I confided in you. Trust me enough to do the same. Tell me. *Love me.*"

Matt, she ached to cry. *Matt, if only you knew how desperate I am to give you that and more. If only . . .*

Those two words seemed to define her life when she needed something real and good. She *had* to have this moment, a too-small slice of time and unity, if she could have nothing else.

With shaking fingers she slid a button free from his shirt. He caught her wrist and stilled her hand.

"Why?" he demanded roughly. "If you're trying to placate me, forget it. Baring some skin isn't what I need from you."

"You do need it, Matthew. And so do I. Let me touch you, taste you. While you feel and see me."

"I told you that unless there's commitment, we can't—"

She silenced him with her mouth full on his. When she drew back, Dee knew that she'd increased his ardor sufficiently to take her offering, a paltry substitute for his greater demand. She had to be careful, but she hadn't the heart or will to deny them a closer bonding.

"No consummation tonight, Matthew. But *we* both need more than friendship and kisses. For now, the only thing standing between us that matters is your shirt."

Ten

"Hold my glass." He thrust it into Dee's unsteady grip, then scooped her into his arms with an impatience matched by his stride.

"Where are you—"

"We're taking this to your bedroom. I have no intentions of dividing my attention between you and listening for a squeak from the upstairs. Got a lock on your door?"

"I . . . yes, but—" Before she could finish he'd turned the lock and tumbled her onto the mattress.

Moonlight spilled through the thin sheath of white curtains, revealing him in shadow. Even if they'd been shuttered in absolute darkness, she would have picked up his unique scent, the sound of his breathing.

His body strained close, calling to her own. But it was his spirit, the intangible force that composed his essence, that she felt most strongly. It exerted a hold over her that went far beyond the realm of the senses.

"Do you have any candles in here that we can use?" His voice was a touch in itself, stroking her in places unseen.

"I wish I did, but no."

"Let there be light anyway." The bedside lamp went on, surrounding them with a soft illumination. "I hope you don't mind, but I have a need to see what I've only been able to imagine."

"Imagine no more." Dee stood—close, but not so close that he couldn't watch her shy yet eager disrobing. The peach silk beneath her fingers gradually parted, each tiny pearl unlooped revealing more to his gaze. He looked torn between wanting to strip her with haste and relishing the anticipation.

Dee made it last. This was a first, and first times could never be repeated. Besides, she wasn't too sure of herself when it came to enticing a man.

She needn't have worried. Matthew's groan of near ecstasy assured her as she dropped her blouse to the floor, followed by a pale lacy bra.

"Sweet heaven," he breathed. "I pictured you in every way imaginable, but the fantasy was nothing like this."

"Do you like what you see?" she asked anxiously.

"Do I like what I see?" His hand hovered a hair's breadth away, so near she could feel their body heat join—then sizzle as he cupped her and slowly squeezed. "No, Dee, I don't like what I see. *I covet it.*"

"And I covet you," she confessed, damning caution. Matthew was, after all, a man who held fast to his principles. Knowing that, she embraced a limited freedom. As long as she didn't give him the commitment he demanded, she was protected, and thus Matthew. They could want, see, feel, and taste. They could almost have it all.

"If you want me, then take off my shirt and see me as a flesh and blood man."

It was all the prompting she needed. As she fumbled with buttons, his hands were divided between massaging her breasts and stroking her nipples.

When she reached the last visible button, her gaze fixed on the straining front of his pants. Dee quickly tugged his shirttail free and finished her priveleged task. Cotton joined silk on the floor.

She stopped. On his chest was a stunning work of needled art.

She traced the sweep of two wings that spanned the generous width of his chest. She saw it centered between the wings and running the length of his breastbone.

"An angel," she whispered.

"With hair."

"Matthew." The feel of that hair was marvelous, and marvelously generous in supply. "It's beautiful."

"Then we have a mutual admiration." He moved decisively, sitting on the edge of her bed, then smoothly pivoting her hips so that she faced him. "Are you nervous?"

"A little."

"So am I. But nervous or assured or anything in between, whatever we share is blessed and good. Straddle my hips and let's put each other at ease."

Though her movements were stiff and a little awkward, she knew what they were doing was so right. The flounce of her black velvet skirt hid the place where they joined, where he pressed hard against her softness.

"Shut your eyes. Shut them. For me."

For him she would do anything. Dee was sealed in darkness as effective as a blindfold. Her senses immediately heightened. The smell of him, of her, of the anticipation between them was erotic and thick.

He reached for the glass she'd set on the nightstand, bringing his chest flush with hers. She felt the pounding of her heart meet his. She heard the clinking of ice cubes. And then she gasped.

Sharply bracing, the frozen liquid traced a single areola, then tapped against the contracted tip of her nipple. It became as hard as his bound erection, which he began to rub and slightly thrust.

When she thought she could stand the acute stimulation no longer, he stopped and blew a warm stream of air back and forth against the chill he'd created. She shivered uncontrollably.

"Cold? Or hot?"

"Yes . . . no. Both." Indeed, she was freezing. She was burning up.

"But you do like it, don't you? If not, I'll stop."

"Don't stop. I love it."

"And I love you. No, don't open your eyes. I want them closed. I want this show of trust from you. If you can't give it to me any other way, I'll take it like this."

She did let him take it. In his exotic torture, the glide of a cube over her other breast, the slice of icy wetness sliding up her neck and around her chin, she let him take it. Her temple received equal attention before she felt him stroke down her cheeks, bathing her in wintry tears.

Even in her mad flight she hadn't felt so totally defenseless, at the mercy of a man's strong will. There was an indomitable power in Matthew. In whatever he did or said she always sensed its presence, but never more than now.

The clinking of ice to glass again. Then came the broad stroke of his palm to her chest. Like a master painter in an artistic frenzy, he swept the cube over her skin until the ice was but a shrunken pebble cinching a taut nipple against his thumb.

Before she could cry out from the pleasure, of the exotic freezing burn, he joined his chest with hers and shared his body's heat, feverishly rubbing, then tenderly pressing. His hands were wet, still cold, as they spanned her back and held her tightly against him.

"Feel my heart, Dee. Feel it beating fast but steady. Do you feel it?"

"I do feel it." She shivered and he held her more tightly. "And Matthew, I need it more than you could know."

"Then open your eyes."

His face was close, intense. Searching hers.

"My heart, beloved, is like the rest of me. Imperfect. Impure. But open and wiser for its mistakes. Whatever the condition, it does beat for you. I am so in love with you. Please, Dee, tell me you feel it too."

Was she in love?

Did an angel have wings?

"Matthew."

His name was a broken sob. A plea to heaven. His name was all she dared say because if she spoke her heart, nothing would be left unsaid. Not even that Loren and Jason could be stripped from her protective arms and given into the keeping of a brutal man who claimed the custody right of a father. Not even that he was searching for her and would use his far-reaching clout to see her rot behind bars. And Matthew, Matthew was the kind of man who would wage an unwinnable battle. A man who would willingly grow old waiting for a woman who could die young in her sleep before the truth could set her free.

"I love you, Dee. Passionately. Carnally. Every way a man can love a woman, I do love you. Keep your secrets for now if you have to, but commit your love to me. Three words, Dee. Say them."

It wasn't easy, but she met his pleading gaze, thus giving her lie credence. "No. Forgive me, Matthew, but *no.*"

"Then why the tears?"

"Because I wish I could say yes."

He looked deeply hurt. He looked as if her tears were those he'd like to cry himself but wouldn't. Then his eyes narrowed. An expression of determination edged out any sign of acceptance of her statement or sympathy for the position she claimed.

"Maybe you won't say that you love me as I love you. But you do want me and that's something you can't deny." His fingers threaded into her hair before he pulled her forward. "Kiss me. Kiss me, dammit."

"Matt—" Her entreaty was cut off by the crush of his lips. His tongue invaded her mouth voraciously, as if it were seeking out every secret she kept, searching for truths and lies. It was not a nice kiss. It was aggressive and demanding and honest in its anger. Yet it was soulful and sincere, meant to arouse and succeeding.

His chest punished as much as it caressed her bare breasts. And his hands, his hands were the devil's own. In her hair, on her face, between her thighs, over her buttocks before sliding forward. Teasing, tantalizing. Gripping, releasing. She was in agony with each purposeful stroke of intimate pursuit.

When she was reduced to mindless cries for more, he laughed with grim satisfaction.

"More, Dee? You want more? So do I. I want it all. I'm not proud, just desperate. I hurt, Dee. I hurt from wanting you, and it's more than physical. Can you feel it in my hands? Feel them on your body, wanting and willing to grant you anything but release from me. They want to dry every tear you weep and . . . you're crying again. I'm so glad you're crying. Cry for me. Cry for me to be inside you, in every way, inside you."

"You're tearing me apart, Matt. Why are you doing this to me?"

"Ask your heart, not me, for the answer. And

while you're at it, I'm getting rid of your clothes. I want you to feel me under your skin as deeply as you're under mine."

She cried openly as she stood and he peeled off panties and hose and black velvet skirt.

She was nude. Cool air brushed her skin. His mouth tasted her belly, dipped into her navel, then nuzzled the triangle at the apex of her thighs. Her knees gave way. His hands steadied her, then gripped her buttocks.

"Lie down on the bed," he commanded her softly. "Lie down beside me. For me. *Only . . . for . . . me.*"

She wasn't aware that she'd obeyed, only that somehow she was on the bed with Matthew stretched out beside her. They snuggled, face-to-face, knee-to-knee, embracing. Until he skimmed downward, and she clasped his mouth to her breast.

Moist heat enveloped her. He greedily sucked, raked his teeth gently against the peak while she thrust her chest higher, seeking a perfect fit.

"You're made for me." His words vibrated against her skin that was fevered and pulsing. The sudden slide of a testing finger left her writhing, when it burrowed deep inside, her hips rose off the bed.

"Pretend with me," he urged. "Imagine more than this part of me inside you. Pretend it's us, and our bodies are one. Can you feel it? See it? I'm filling you up and you're taking me. The good. The unholy. But you want all of me. You can have it, beloved. The price is your trust."

"I'm dying," she heard herself say. "Matthew, you're killing me."

"Then die the sweetest death at my hands." His hands were no longer the only instrument of his loving destruction. His head moved between her legs and his moving, sensual torment drove her to piteous whimpers for his tender mercy.

He lay on top of her, laced their fingers together, then spread her arms.

"Profess your love for me, Dee. Your lie of omission is depriving us both of what we need. Tonight and beyond."

"Don't—don't love you," she gasped out. When he released her hands, she entreated him with the rising of her hips, the clench of her nails into his back. He grunted in satisfaction, then wooed her with a slow buck and grind that made her strain for more than a mock coupling. Never had she felt such wondrous sensations. Never had she hurt with such a horrible emptiness.

"Beg for my love," he demanded. "Beg me to give you what you won't give me."

"Love me," she cried, her resistance all but dissolved by his teasing thrusts. "I'm begging you to say that you love me. Matthew, let it be enough."

His laugh was triumphant. "I do love you, Dee. Enough not to be where I belong. Inside you, all the way inside you. That's how deep my love goes." He moved against her once more, before plunging two fingers deep where he'd sworn by his love not to enter.

She orgasmed. Her muscles went taut, then quivered with the frenzy of sensations. Her many cries of his name were greedily swallowed by his mouth. It was beautiful, poetic in its pain. But what she experienced went beyond the physical. His was the absolute claiming of her soul, the ultimate violation of her emotional safety.

"Why?" she sobbed, feeling his fingers gently trace her tears. "Why did you do this to me, Matthew?"

"Because I love you. Because you tried to make me believe that you don't love me."

She raised her hand to his face. Her heart was breaking. It was breaking because they had crossed the line from what they had been to lovers. It was breaking because she loved him more than ever. He was the one man she could marry, spend her life with and thank God for each day he filled her existence. For that reason, she had to remain silent. For that reason, of all the men in the world, he was the one she must not take.

But when she felt the hardness in him, she knew that she couldn't turn away from him yet.

She slid a hand between them and fondled him. "Let me, Matthew. Let me give *you* ease."

"No." His refusal was quick and final, as unyielding as the flesh he denied her.

"And is this because you love me?"

"This is because . . ." He kissed her hard and completely, then got up. "Because I won't compromise on this any more than I won't on what I want from you."

"You're leaving?" she asked in disbelief as he reached for his shirt. "You can't leave me now."

"I never leave you, Dee. Even when you can't see me I'm there." Matthew regarded her long and desirously before he quickly covered her up with a comforter.

Dee was beyond speech, beyond anything but the need to bring him back into her arms. Until Matthew was already unlocking the door. "But— but where are you going?"

"To church."

"To church? You're leaving me like this to go to church? Matthew, please. Come back."

"While I'm at church I'll still be here," he assured her. "Just think about me, about what we've shared, and I'm that close to you. But right now I'm in need of some serious prayer. Any requests while I'm there?"

"Yes. Ask why a man leaves a naked woman he says he loves. Ask why he won't let her give him even a partial satisfaction."

"I don't have to check with anyone to tell you that. I won't ever be satisfied until you give me all that you are. Your secrets. Fears. Hopes and dreams. At least tonight you gave me enough to sustain my faith in us. I can wait for the rest."

"You could get tired of waiting, Matt."

He speared her with a look that made her shake. It was all-knowing, as if he saw through her and could read her thoughts while his own remained a mystery.

"Judging from tonight, I doubt it. I will get that commitment from you—and once given, we'll seal our vows." His gaze roved over her. "Think about it, Dee. Making love for hours. Tangled legs and rumpled sheets. *Sex* . . . shared—endless pleasures."

Eleven

Two days later, early on Saturday morning, Matt
received a phone call. He sat straighter in bed as
he listened to Sally Henderson's recounting of her
mother breaking her hip on Thanksgiving, and,
Reverend, so sorry to call with the Christmas
cantata at stake, but as the only child of a widow,
she'd be out of town indefinitely tending dear
Mother. Matthew offered his usual calming words,
then hung up.

"Yes!" he whooped, raising a victory fist. *Your
will be done, Father. I hope the mother gets well.
But if it takes a while, I could use the time on this
end. And I won't waste a second. I'm on the mission even as we speak.*

Without so much as a concluding amen, Matt
strode naked to the kitchen and went to the
freezer. Glass in hand, he returned to his bed, and
grabbed the phone.

"Hello?"

"Love the husky voice. Anyone ever tell you how
sexy you sound first thing in the morning?"

Dee's sleep-laden murmur sounded like a no.
He wished that were true, though reason denied
the possibility.

"I missed you yesterday," she said with a yawn. Once she woke beside him each morning, he would cover her yawns with a kiss. "How did things turn out at the hospital?"

"I'm afraid one of the Smith kids didn't make it. Because of that wreck, Andy won't be scribbling in the hymnal tomorrow."

"That poor family, they must be grieving terribly."

"They are. It was a long day and night for the Smiths."

"And for you, Matt."

"Yes," he agreed somberly. "Dealing with a tragedy like that is hard for me too, but I'm glad I was there to give what little help I could. I'm conducting the funeral Monday. I know you're not very close with the family, but I'm sure they would appreciate your presence. I would too."

"I'll be there. I only wish I could have been there for you when you got home last night."

"Then we share the same wish." A wish that might come true quicker now that some additional ammunition had come his way. "But that's not the reason I called. I just got word of a job opening for a pianist. Think you might be interested?"

"Would I! Where is it? When can I apply?"

"You can apply this morning. It's an opportunity that needs filling immediately."

"Wonderful. Do you have any idea how much it pays?"

He'd suspected Dee was running short of money. Even though he couldn't offer her as much as he wanted to—and would once their incomes cozied up in a joint bank account—he was glad to do what he could for the present.

"Not much, unfortunately. But I do understand the benefits are great. I happen to know who's hiring and he's a super guy, very understanding, and easy to work with. He's supposed to be at the church in an hour or so. Think you could be there for an audition?"

"As soon as we hang up I'm in the tub and getting ready."

Matthew imagined her submerged in the water, a vision that caused an immediate reaction under the covers.

"But you're in bed now, aren't you?" His voice was seductive.

"Yes," she whispered hesitantly.

"So am I." He paused, allowing her imagination to aid his ploy before stirring the flame. "I sleep in the raw . . . but I remember that you wear a nightgown. Is your bedroom door shut?"

"Yes." The sound of her swallowing carried over the wires. Matthew was no less than delighted with her quick response.

"Good. Do something for me? Describe what you're wearing."

"It's a—a long white flannel nightgown. With pink satin ribbons tied in front."

"Ah . . . I can almost see it. The way it's twisted at your hips from your moving in the night, and the flannel on your bare skin as smooth and warm as my palms. But wouldn't you be more comfortable without anything on?"

"Yes," she gasped. "Matthew, what are you—"

"Take it off. Feel the ribbons, Dee, so nice and silky between your fingers. Are they shaking? Yes? That's good. Especially with your eyes closed, and you pretending it's me tugging them loose. Feel my hands on your shoulders, sliding the nightgown from your body. It is off now, isn't it?"

A breathy moan was her answer.

"Imagine me stroking your breasts. Do it for me since I'm not there?"

"Matt—Matt, I've never—"

"You will do it, won't you? For me. Because you

love me and you know how perfectly we'll fit." He blew softly into the receiver and was rewarded with a tortured groan. "Pretend that you've said those three magic words and we're making love. Can you feel me touch you, how your breasts are responding to my mouth?"

"*Lord* . . . oh, my . . . *oh* . . ."

"Ah, Dee. They're so soft. Luscious. Now, listen." Suppressing a groan of his own, Matthew lifted the ice-filled glass close to the receiver. He shook the cubes. "The ice, beloved. Do you hear the ice? You must, since I can hear you moaning. The ice is sliding between my fingers. Cold, so cold on your skin."

"Hot," she gasped. "So . . . hot . . ."

"Mmm. And *wet*." He jiggled the glass once more, then blew a stream of air into the mouthpiece. "Enjoy your bath, Dee. And one other thing—"

"Ah . . . ah, sweet heaven, Matthew—what?"

"I love you." He sent her a parting kiss before murmuring, "See you at church."

He hung up before she could come down from the state of arousal he'd left her in. Stretching broadly, with a grin just as wide, Matt patted the empty space beside him. He could almost forget his own extreme discomfort when he considered his ruse bringing Dee that much closer to filling another open position: Wife.

"The gloves are off, Dee," he said. "Your new employer's ready to play hard ball. And lady, you ain't seen nothin' yet."

As Dee played the postlude, she watched Matthew descend from the pulpit. He caught her gaze, one that mirrored the yearning she felt inside. A sense of connection, of oneness, passed between them before he broke it to touch a member's drooped shoulder. Taking someone else's hand, nodding his head to another, he slowly made his way outside.

The piano keys seemed to respond to the many emotions he evoked in her. The music flowed as everyone stood and exchanged hugs or words of sorrow for the Smiths. Matthew had spoken of life, of humanity's relationship with death, and had given her a new perspective on it.

She'd learned something as she'd listened, rapt, to his message. He believed that death and dying were extensions of life and living, and his words were so convincing, so soothing, she found her bitterness softening.

She'd endured such a terrible blow when Alexis had died. But Matthew, though unaware of her loss, had eased her rage at the horrible injustice of it all.

As Dee struck the last chord, warm palms smoothed over her shoulders. "I sent Jason and Loren home to set the table," Matthew said. "For four, since I invited myself over. They were more than happy to volunteer."

"You're kidding me." Swiveling on the piano stool, she saw that his cheeks were ruddy from the cold. She touched them. Like ice. *Ice.* Her own cheeks flared hotly. "Usually they argue about who takes the duty. How you do it, Matthew, I don't know. But whatever the means, I'm glad it works."

"Bribery. Shameless bribery. I happened to mention that after lunch I need help picking out your Christmas tree. You can come too—for a price."

"Clearing the table?"

"No, dessert. I'd like dessert after they're asleep. Something sweet and delicious."

"You must mean the divinity I made."

"Wrong again. *Ice—*" He chuckled wickedly when Dee moaned. All she had to imagine to burn with need was the clink of cubes in a glass. "—Cream," he added, laughing.

"Rev. Peters, you are a very sneaky man."

"Uh-huh. And a very needy man too." The glide of his palms down her arms was exciting. "I need you tonight, Dee. This evening I have to attend Andy's wake. While I'm there I'd like to know you're waiting for me."

She wanted to tell him that she would willingly wait each and every night they lived. She wanted to tell him she fell more in love with him with each passing day. She compromised and let her eyes say what she couldn't.

"Yes, Matthew. I'll be there for you tonight."

His somber gaze lightened at the promise. "With dessert?"

"Not only are you sneaky, you are impossible."

"But not a bad employer, huh?"

"That was sneaky too. But . . . you're okay."

"Okay?" he protested. "I'm great! The best. How many guys do you know who'd plan to attend each choir practice when they're not even singing in the Christmas program?"

"You didn't mention that yesterday. I hope this doesn't mean we have to perform to your standards of approval." Unable to resist, Dee added meaningfully, "Especially knowing how uncompromising your standards are."

"Touché," he said, grinning.

Arm in arm they went to gather their coats. Matthew helped Dee into hers, his arms wrapping possessively around her once she had it on. "I could get used to seeing you at the piano every Sunday. We make a good team, you and me."

Swallowing hard, she broke free and pushed open the door. Chilly wind caused her eyes to smart, and she was thankful to have winter to blame for the tears that blurred her vision.

In silence they walked across the street to join

Loren and Jason, who were coming to depend as heavily on Matt as she was. Matthew, the strongest man she'd ever known, needed her. Their relationship was growing more complex by the day—and it was twisting her up.

Glancing behind them, Dee saw the two sets of footprints they'd made, placed side by side. She couldn't help but liken them to how close she and Matt had become. But snow melted with the changing of seasons.

She and Matthew. Like footprints in the snow.

Twelve

"'We wish you a merry Christmas . . .'" All evening long Dee's and Matt's voices had blended in perfect harmony, but the same couldn't be said for those of the rest of the Christmas eve carolers.

There were sixteen of them, and everyone was huddled close outside the last house they were visiting. Dee, standing in front of Matt, jumped when she felt a light squeeze on her behind. Turning just far enough to shoot Matt a warning glare, she noticed he was looking over her head and smiling as innocently as an angel. She couldn't help but grin herself.

Dee had never felt happier in her life, and it was with great joy that she sang the rest of the song, then shouted "Merry Christmas!" along with the others.

As soon as the group broke up for their private celebrations, she and Matthew and the two children turned for home. A few blocks shy, Matt and Jason darted to a pile of snow.

"It's the boys against the girls," they crowed before Matt pitched the first snowball, which hit Dee's back. She yelped in feigned outrage, then she and Loren ran for the cover of a huge spruce tree. A fight ensued, with all four getting covered with snow. Matthew ended the jubilant brawl by storming the tree and pouncing on Dee. They tumbled to the ground with Matthew on top.

Dee was still laughing when she noticed his face was inches from hers, the white puffs of her breath mingling with his. He was pressed intimately between her legs and fully aroused.

"I'd kiss you," he said hoarsely, "except there's no mistletoe." He bounded up, then helped her to her feet. As he was brushing her off, he whispered, "Besides, where I want most to kiss you isn't permissible in public places."

"That's . . . kinky," she whispered back.

He swiped a snowflake from her nose. "Just think, Dee, we could be kinky and live on the edge of danger together ever after."

Dee forced herself to laugh and hid her flinch by turning away from him and facing the children. "Who wants to put out cookies and milk for Santa?"

"Cookies and milk for Santa," they repeated, groaning. "Aw, c'mon, Dee, we haven't done something that dumb in years."

"No," she said, still off balance. "No, of course not. But this year is different. Matt's sharing Christmas with us."

"And I agree with the kids that's a dumb idea," Matt chimed in. "But leaving a spread like sausage and cheese and champagne, that's more like it. Takes more time than cookies and milk though, so the sooner you kids get to work, the sooner you'll be in bed and have Saint Nick parking his sleigh at your door. That is . . . unless you're too old for him to put his presents under the tree?"

"No way! I'm going home." Jason was already running.

Loren looked at the two adults. "No hanky-panky now," she singsonged before following Jason.

Matthew quirked a brow.

Dee shook her head. "Sometimes I wonder if we're too affectionate in front of them, Matt. I don't want us to be a bad influence."

"We're good for them. *I'm* good for them," he asserted, reminding her of yet another reason she needed him in her life. "And it's healthy for kids to see two adults show they care for each other."

They'd started walking, his arm around her shoulders, but now Matthew slowed his pace to a stop. "Didn't they ever see your—your . . ." He had trouble getting the word out. "Did your husbands, either of them, display affection toward you?"

"No," she quickly answered.

"You never talk about them. Why not?"

"Because I don't like to remember."

"For once I wish you would. I have a need to know, Dee."

"And I have a need to forget. I don't want to taint what we have by dredging up old memories."

"Do they keep in touch?" Matt persisted, driven by a compulsion to dig into her past at the same time that he shunned the thought of other men intimately knowing and loving the only woman he'd ever wanted to share his life with. "I half expected to see their dad show up bearing gifts since there aren't any with his name as the giver under the tree. Even distant fathers often send Christmas presents—to salve their conscience or whatever."

He felt her shoulders tense. When Dee spoke, her voice seemed guarded, on edge.

"These men, Matthew, they're . . . not like you."

"Then, what *are* they like?" He wanted to ask what they were like in and out of bed. Why she'd divorced one and chosen no better with the other. He gritted his teeth while questions and jealousy crowded to get out.

"I want to know about their father," he said when Dee remained silent. "I want to know why you married him, divorced him. What he does for a living, and why the kids don't have so much as a trinket to show for his existence under the tree. I want to know who your second husband was and why the children don't even mention his name."

"Matthew, stop." Dee wouldn't look at him, but if her eyes matched her voice, they were pleading. "It doesn't matter."

"It matters greatly to me. You're a fine and gifted woman, Dee, and what you are now doesn't mesh with who you must have been." He tried to force her to meet his probing gaze, but her eyes darted away. "Help me to understand. Tell me what kind of parents would let their daughter be sucked into a harmful relationship and have two babies by the time she was seventeen. Didn't they love you? Didn't they care?"

"Of course they loved me," she said in their defense. "They've always cared. And they still care for . . . him."

"Him. Jason and Loren's father. What was he, a kid himself, some horny nitwit who didn't know how to use a damn rubber? Or was he older, able to seduce a young girl and blind her parents to something so wrong?"

"He's much older than me."

"I thought so. And he's rich, isn't he?"

"How could you know that?" she demanded.

"The kids come from money. Once when we were having canned salmon patties for dinner, I heard Loren mutter something under her breath about missing having a cook."

Dee's sigh sounded of relief. "Okay, so what? Having been rich is not a crime."

"No, but molestation is. Tell me, did he buy off your parents to gain a child bride and hush a scandal?" Something suddenly occurred to Matt. Why hadn't he thought of it before? "Were you ever married to *him*?"

"No," she said haltingly. "No, Vince and I were never married."

"Ah, Vince. *He* has a name. What about the other one? A name, Dee, I want a name."

"Nick. All right, Nick!" She visibly shuddered. "Enough questions, no more."

"I want to know everything there is to know about this scum named Vince. Then you can get to Nick. How long you were together, how he treated you—"

"Nick's a lawyer. A sleazeball lawyer. That's all I'm telling you and it's more than I should have."

She darted off, making it as far as the parsonage before he caught up with her. He grabbed her arm and pulled her into the shadows. They were both breathing hard, the cold air burning their throats. Matthew's burned even more from the questions he finally refused to choke back.

"I keep telling myself that any day you'll trust me. Trust me now, Dee. Give me a piece of your past so we can get on with our future. It's time we moved forward."

"We have no future, Matt. Not the kind you want or deserve." She pushed at his chest, but he refused to move. "Let me go. You can come with me or you can go it alone. Either way I'm not giving you any answers."

His rage was swift and deep. He'd never shaken a woman before, but at the moment he wanted to shake every detail about her life loose from her head.

"You tell me we have no future and expect me to let you go with that? Haven't you learned anything about me, or at least guessed I've only been biding my time before calling your bluff? You love me." He did shake her then. "You love me, dammit. And tonight you're saying those three words, even if you confess nothing else."

"No!" When she struggled against him, he locked her in his arms. "I can't. I won't. And you can't force it from me."

"You can. You will. And I won't have to force what's already there."

"No—no, I feel nothing—"

"You're running, Dee. If not from them, then from what you feel for me. You feel love. You feel *this*." He placed a hand over the juncture of her thighs. "You're wet."

"It's from the snow when we fell."

"Then you don't need to worry about me making sure that this isn't another one of your lies."

He pulled her inside his house, then tugged off a glove with his teeth. There in the dark hallway, he breached her pants and probed her intimately with a finger.

Her legs nearly buckled. "Don't want you," she cried. "Can't want you, Matthew—"

"But you do. Here. And now."

He was through being patient. He was through waiting for disclosures. Adhering to principles had brought him to the edge of human endurance. "Undo my pants," he whispered sharply.

He knew a horrible moment when she hesitated, but then her hand reached toward him. As she slid down his zipper, he could feel her hand tremble. They were both shaking and he knew it had little to do with the cold. In this they were partners, as they were in all else.

And in doing this he would make Dee see the perfection of their bond.

Thirteen

Matthew stopped her long enough to get rid of their remaining gloves and drop them to the floor. They resumed their urgent search of skin beneath sweaters, and their lips met in a rapacious kiss. His breath filled her mouth in a rush as he guided her hand to touch him. It was a tentative touch, eager yet oddly unsure for a woman of her experience. But she had said her other men were unlike him. He wanted the reassurance that *especially* in this, that was true.

"Wrap your fingers around me," he urgently commanded. "As tight as you're meant to hold me inside."

"Tell me what you want," she whispered. "Is this right?"

"Is it right?" He might have laughed at the question if he weren't seriously worried about his slipping control. "Everything about us is right. Except for what you keep from me." Including the absence of her vow that would sanctify what he could no longer wait for.

Matthew took her hand out of his pants, certain that when he took her he would feel no guilt, no sense of having committed a wrong act. When he stripped off his coat and laid it down, she said anxiously, "I can give you what you've given me before without us lying down."

"No, Dee. This is for keeps, for real. And I want nothing between my flesh and yours."

He peeled her pants to her knees and did the same with his own. "Now lie down and know me as a man, Delilah. A man who refuses to wait any longer to love you in the most intimate way a man and a woman can."

When she hesitated, he guided himself between her thighs. She was sleek, ready. She slumped to the floor, clutching his shirt, pulling him down with her.

"Say you need me inside you as much as I need to be there."

"Yes. *Yes.*"

"Then take me." He penetrated her, but not deeply. Dee was softly moaning, her head slightly thrashing. "I want to honor your body with mine," he said, groaning and silently praying for control so he could hang on long enough to give her everything she deserved.

"Honor and . . . cherish with my body . . ." *I pledge to wed thee.* "I love you. And in my heart I'll love you always. With all that is in me"—*All that is good, all that is noble, all that is imperfect and too human*—"I give to you now. I am yours, beloved." *As you are mine. Now and forever.*

He wooed his bride with shallow thrusts, fighting his body's demand to plunge deeply. But then he lost the battle and thrust his hips forward, only to find her resistant.

Dee cried out, a cry that might have been of pleasure or pain. Almost out of his mind, he wondered if he was imagining the too-tight walls squeezing out what little sanity he still possessed. His body was in agony, while her own wasn't keeping up with the momentum of unleashed desire.

"There's something wrong," he gasped out. "You're too tight. Dee, tell me you want this. I'd never force—" He pulled out with the help of a force greater than himself.

"Don't stop! It's right. Never more right." Her hips were arching, her body pleading while he searched for lost reason. His fingers went to the source that had stopped his unstoppable purpose, making her cry out in a long, keening sound and dig her nails into his buttocks. *"Love me."*

She seemed half crazed, writhing beneath him, and then he felt her trying to put him back inside her. It wouldn't be fair of him to make the demand when she was so focused on the need to mate. But he was desperate enough to use her weakness to make her speak what he knew to be true.

"Love *me*," he said urgently, turning her words on her. "Say you love me. Once is all it'll take for you to feel me inside."

"I . . ." She hesitated, and he pressed a little harder against her. "*I love you.* Dear God, I do."

Her sleek but resisting chamber took his forceful plunge. She shrieked into his mouth at the exact moment he felt his most sensitive flesh hit the tip of her womb.

Why was she so tight? Why had she made that sharp cry? No, it *couldn't* be. He must have imagined . . . It was just that it had been so long since he'd been with a woman that . . .

Before he could thrust a second time to test the possibility of the impossible, his body began to pulsate and jerk. Somehow he commanded himself to withdraw. But without even a moment to savor what he'd been driven to claim, he spasmed and warm liquid pooled between his palm and her navel.

He cursed his body's impatience. He railed at

his irresponsible, compulsive entry without protection. And as he stroked her abdomen, he wanted to cry bitter tears for his inability to join himself and this woman with a thousand deep thrusts.

He'd waited a lifetime for Dee, and it had seemed an eternity that he'd denied their mating, and for what? This. This lesson in humility. A frantic coupling culminating in a single plunge he could have sworn almost tore her apart. What they'd shared was sacred to him. And vastly unfulfilling. If she was half as unsatisfied as he, the moans Dee was making had to be those of frustration.

Quickly, he gave her the paltry substitution of fingers for what was now spent. She cried his name again and again while he stared down at her in the dark. His mate was sensitive, generous to the point where he suspected she might fake pleasure to soothe his hurt pride. As he thought of this, his pride hurt worse.

"I'm sorry, Dee," he said quietly. "Forgive me, it's just been so long, and I love you so much and—"

"Matthew, Matthew." She was laughing and crying at once. "Thank you. Thank . . . thank you."

"I'll make it up to you. I'll—huh?"

"That was the most—the most beautiful, unforgettable experience of my life. I . . . I thank you."

Matthew considered this remarkable woman. So remarkable he'd ask her to marry him in a heartbeat if she'd give him a single sign of acceptance.

A woman so remarkable she was covering his face with kisses for the worst sexual performance of his life, which only strengthened his suspicion that her secrets went deeper than he'd ever guessed. Unless . . . Vince and Nick had been built like Ken dolls. Maybe that was it. Or it could be that Dee's other men had been real duds in the sack. He could almost accept that convoluted explanation easier than the idea that she'd been a virgin.

"I wish it had been better for you." His battered ego fished for reassurance even as he cast for clues.

"Better?" Dee hugged him tight and wrapped her legs even tighter around his. "How could it be better than this? I love you, Matthew," she said in a rush. "I *do* love you."

He cherished her vow, and her happiness took some of the sting out of their too-brief consummation. Yet he couldn't disregard the fact that something was definitely out of sync.

"Let me make sure I have this straight. Are you saying that making love with me was the best you've ever had?"

"The best. The absolute, most incredible best. I never dreamed, never guessed it could be like this."

Matthew was glad the darkness hid his frown. Perhaps it was the emotional bonding, the intensity of mutual need so long denied that had evoked such an unlikely remark. But he didn't think so. His suspicions were growing stronger.

"If this was your best," he said carefully, "I can't wait to show you how good it can get."

Dee went still; he sensed her weighing their exchange.

"I'm getting cold all of a sudden." She began tugging at her pants, and he rolled off her. He would have extended their intimacy by gently assisting her as she dressed, but she jerked her clothes back into place. Unable to miss that she was suddenly eager to leave, he got up and quickly fixed his own clothes. Dee stood, not waiting for him to offer a hand.

She swayed, and he caught her.

"Are you okay?"

"Fine. I'm fine. Thank you, Matthew," she said politely. He didn't like her subtle withdrawal any more than he cared for his quick joining with this woman he would claim as his wife. One who continued to boggle his mind.

Her sweet kiss to his cheek didn't soothe his anxiety. Matt hauled her against him and kissed her possessively before picking up the coat that had been their prenuptial bed.

As they walked to her house, she snuggled beneath his arm, granting them the closeness she'd broken with her urgency to leave.

Once inside the living room, dark but for the twinkling lights on the tree, Dee went to check on the children.

"All's well?" he asked when she returned.

"They're sound asleep. And they left out a feast for Santa in the kitchen. You go ahead and sample the treats. I'll join you after I take a hot bath."

"I'd rather we take a hot shower together and pick up where we left off."

"We'd—we'd better not."

"Why not?" he countered quickly. "They're sleeping soundly and we can keep our whispers low. Santa's helper has had a rest and he's ready to give Mrs. Claus a memorable present. Let's light some candles and lock the bathroom door. My fingers are itching to unwrap one delicious package."

"Next time." She brushed his lips with a kiss, then moved away before he could lock her against him. "Uncork the champagne? I'll be quick so we can celebrate."

He wanted to ask her if she meant Christmas or their lovemaking. If it was the latter, she could use some pointers in how to extend the afterglow. But he deemed it wise to keep his thoughts to himself until he sorted out what was going on.

He heard the faint sound of her singing over the

rush of water. My, didn't she sound like a woman who'd been well bedded and loved. It seemed to him that apparently she didn't realize how lacking their slam-bam-brrr-I'm-cold-now-and-thank-you-sir coupling had been.

Matt went to the kitchen, wondering how in the world he was going to explain his suspicions about her virginity. He saw the makings of a romantic conclusion to what they'd barely started: Champagne. Cheese and sausage and crackers. Mistletoe.

He lifted the sprig, then dropped it.

He turned his hands up, then down, under the light, staring at the fingertips that had moved inside her, seeking to satisfy.

"I see it but I still can't believe it," he whispered. He unzipped his pants and sought concurring proof. Next he shrugged out of his coat and closely examined the faintly tinged lining.

A virgin. Sweet heaven above, she *had* been a virgin, which meant that barring virgin births, Jason and Loren weren't hers.

Should he confront her while she was defenseless in the tub? Would she give in, tell the truth, and explain a situation that had to be far more complex than he'd ever imagined?

Matthew debated with himself. He said a silent prayer, seeking some much-needed guidance. The answer he received called for a patience he wasn't feeling. And yet he knew the answer was right.

He had to build on what he and Dee had established until she confided what he was sure was a serious intrigue involving two men: A lawyer and a wealthy father who were after a woman neither had married.

But *he* would. In his mind they were as good as legally bound. He took Dee's side in whatever had driven her to commit what had to be a desperate, dangerous, and illegal act.

After assuring himself that she was still in the tub, Matt quickly went to the kitchen sink and washed. Hands. Coat. And the instrument responsible for the bloodstains on all three.

As the last traces of evidence drained away, Matthew felt he'd granted Dee what protection he could for the moment. The problem lay in protecting her from herself while she tried to shield him with her silence.

Fourteen

"Ho, ho, ho, Santa. You have been a very naughty boy." Dee withdrew the filmy black negligee nestled in a purple-tissue-lined box. "You didn't buy this around here, did you? I've been working hard on improving my reputation, and yours wouldn't be sterling if someone caught you picking out this."

"I found it at a boutique last month when I was out of town. Do you like it?" His intimate smile set off an explosion of elation inside her, and she tingled from the roots of her hair to the soles of her feet. With his shirt unbuttoned and the snap of his jeans undone, he made a very sexy Santa.

They snuggled in the middle of her bed, their gifts for each other piled at the foot. "It's beautiful, Matthew. And very risqué. I love it."

"And you love me," he said huskily.

"You know that I do." She'd given him, after all, what he had insisted she would. Dee felt a bittersweet joy in that, quickly reminding herself that at least they had cherished memories no one could ever take away. Including the loss of her virtue. How she regretted that he hadn't known—would never know. And yet she was grateful that the obstacle that had kept her from expressing one certain truth had disappeared.

"I'm glad you appreciate this bit of nothing." He grinned. "After all, I did work up a sweat searching through a bunch of racks while the saleswoman kept holding up garter belts. When she started pulling out novelty panties I grabbed this so I could get out of there before she suggested handcuffs."

"You mean you didn't get me a pair?" Dee laughed, shutting her mind to thoughts of their precarious future. The night was magic, and so was the slight burning sensation between her legs.

"I'll save the accessories for next year," he murmured. Her high spirits took a quick dip. Would there be a next year? "Try it on for me?"

Dee hugged him tightly as a feeling of desperation rose in her. For now he was hers, completely hers. She clung to him before letting go and slowly disrobing. The wisp of black silk floated down her body, touching her where she needed his hands to be.

"You wear it well," he said with approval. "So well I don't think you should put it on except when I'm the only one around."

"You're not afraid I'll wear it to church tomorrow for your Christmas sermon? You know me, Ms. Jezebel."

"And Mr. Holier-Than-Thou knows better now that the evidence is in. . . ." His emphasis on *evidence* made her stiffen. "The lady in red's closer to an angel in white."

"I'll change before the kids wake up," she said, feeling uneasy. "This can be our little secret."

"Secrets," he mused. Matthew tapped a finger to his lips. "I like sharing secrets with you. Saying things in private that no one else knows. It's . . . intimate. Something between the two of us that's built on trust. And you can trust me, Dee. I would never betray you, don't you know?"

"Sometimes, Matt, your support seems like the one constant in my life. You've earned my trust."

But she hadn't earned his, her conscience taunted. She had deceived him from the beginning. Even as their bodies had joined, she'd deceived him. Matthew deserved only honesty, and she'd given him precious little of it. If she could ever give him the whole truth, would he love her as much? Would he be able trust her then?

"You look sad. Can you tell me why, or is that a secret you're not willing to share?"

"I'm sad because you have to go home tonight while I sleep alone in my bed. Keeping up appearances—bah, humbug." Dee forced a bright smile and reached for a package. "I have a gift for you, but I'm afraid it's not nearly as extravagant as the one you gave me."

Matthew shook the box and made several outlandish guesses as to its contents. It turned out to be a pair of slippers.

"They're me. Definitely me." He wriggled his toes while Dee slipped them on his feet.

"I wish I could have afforded more," she confessed. "Unfortunately, my budget was a little tight this year."

"What you gave me tonight was the most precious gift a woman can give to a man." Dee's gaze flew to his, and her heart began to beat too fast. Gently he touched his hand to her cheek. "You said that you loved me, and, beloved, that means more to me than any store-bought present."

He stroked her hair before pulling her onto his lap and hugging her. "And besides, how did you know I always wanted slippers that look like fluffy teddy bear feet? *Raaarh*." Matt feasted on her neck, then reached for the coat he'd tossed on the floor.

Why did the lining appear damp? Surely what snow they'd gotten on it should have dried by now. When he stroked it, a sudden tension seemed to fill the room and a buzz sounded in her head. Then he smiled and withdrew a small, fancy wrapped package from a pocket.

Air returned to her lungs. Dee could almost forget the strange moment when she opened a black velvet jeweler's box and touched the slender gold chain.

"An ankle bracelet?"

Matthew nodded. "I also looked at rings while I was at the boutique."

She knew better than to ask what kind but couldn't resist. "Dinner rings?"

"No. Two gold rings. His and hers with diamonds forming crosses. Stand up for me."

She followed his command. Wedging her foot between the tops of his thighs, he fastened the chain, then tumbled her back onto the bed.

"Don't move," he said firmly before slipping free from her arms and going out the door. When he returned, he clicked the lock and knelt beside her, holding a bright red plastic ice tray in his hands.

"I saved the best present for last. I put it in your freezer when I came by to pick you guys up for the caroling. They're not quite frozen, but they are awfully cute. Little Santa Claus–shaped cubes." He placed one in his mouth, then fed it to her. "Merry Christmas, Mrs. Claus, from the mister."

She groaned. "For a minister you certainly have an innovative approach to satisfying your libido. Did they teach you sensual torture in the seminary?"

He didn't smile at her jest. She wasn't sure if he'd even heard her. He seemed distant. Was he thinking, praying . . . plotting?

Without warning, Matt crouched between her legs.

"Open them," he whispered. "Yes, yes . . . like that." The gentle probing of his fingertip created another kind of anxiety. "Tender?" he asked in a soft, caring voice.

"Yes—no. Matthew, quit looking at me there."

"I've looked at you there before, though maybe you were beyond caring. Don't be self-conscious with me now. We have been as close as two people can get. Almost, anyway. I understand sharing the birth of a baby is the ultimate in intimacy. Considering how small you turned out to be, I can't help but wonder if you had a hard time delivering?"

Dee's breath caught when he stroked her once with a cube, then flicked the heat of his tongue against the same spot.

"N-no," she stammered. "Not too—too hard."

"Then easy labors. Easy enough that you hardly knew you'd had them?"

"I . . . why do you want to know?"

"Because I want to share what I missed. I want to share everything with you. Past. Present. Future." He swiped the cube against her once more. "Does that feel good? Make you a little less sore after the most memorable night of your life? By the way, I've never had one that could compare either. You more than exceeded my expectations."

The inflection of his tone was alarming. Dee sat up and pushed at his shoulders.

"I'm not sore anymore, so you can stop."

"If you say so. I only wanted to make the hurt go away." He stroked her cheek with a wet fingertip. "I want to make all your hurts go away. But I can't do that unless you tell me what they are."

She shut her eyes tightly so she wouldn't have to endure his searching gaze. What could she tell him? That she was wanted for kidnapping? Then what? Ask him to make a plea-bargain with heaven or maybe find out if he knew a crackerjack lawyer who could do battle with Nick and the judges Vince had in his pocket? Could the good minister see about getting Alexis raised from the dead so she could point a bony finger at her murdering husband and get Dee off the hook?

Right, Dee, tell him where it hurts. Tell him so he can be as deep in this horrible thing as you are. Maybe he'll even insist on going to the authorities for protection when you found out the hard way how crooked some of them operate.

"It hurts where you had me," she said, desperate for him to drive it all away. "I'm hurting for wanting you back, Matthew." She tried to smile, but failed. "You know how I get when you bring out the ice."

For a minute he said nothing. "Okay, Dee." His sigh was filled with resignation. "If that's the way you want it." Before she could gather her wits he stood beside the bed and stripped off his clothes. "Take a long look and tell me if I measure up to the other men you've seen. And, in this case, feel free to lie."

Dee's throat went dry. He towered over her, lean but muscled, appearing larger than life.

"You're beautiful, Matthew. No one could be more beautiful than you."

"My body's not perfect, but I'm glad it pleases you. Care to see the other tattoo?" He pivoted, revealing a behind that had a pitchfork on one firm mound and a halo on the other.

When he turned back, his face was set in somber lines. "Now we have another little secret, Dee. At the rate we're going, we won't have many left, except any you decide to keep from me. If you're through looking, I'll see what I can do to make at least one hurt go away."

He didn't wait for her answer before returning to the bed. When she reached for the light, he caught her hand.

"Leave it on. No telling what we missed when we made love in the dark."

He laid her down, settling his body on top of hers. "And this time we'll do it right. We'll make it last. Long and greedy and anything but sweet. I'm ready to make up for lost time."

"But—but what if I get pregnant?"

"You love Vince's children, and so do I. Could you actually hate my child and love his?"

"Hate your child? *Our* child? How could you even think such a thing, Matthew?" He had her so off balance with the unexpected turns in his conversation and the aggressiveness of his sensuality. But when his tender, biting kisses began and he rubbed his groin against hers, she could only beg for more than his fleet, cunning fingers.

His penetration was a claiming thrust that left her breathless, and she knew she could never have enough of him. She started to arch her back to pull him in deeper inside her, but he held her still.

"Don't move. Let me feel you a little longer, give you more than I did before. Cheating us like that—I hated it. Especially since it was your first time."

"My first time?" she repeated in a faint voice.

He hesitated, then answered, "With me. Our first time together. There was a lot I wanted to say that didn't get said. Such as how much your sharing yourself intimately meant to me. I want to be sure you realize that sex with this minister is serious business. It's binding."

"How binding?"

"Binding as a contract. More unbreakable than any law."

Contract—there was likely one on her life. Law—she was legally on the wrong side of it. Had he deliberately chosen those terms to test her? But now he was testing her body, retreating, then thrusting.

"That's why if you ever tried to run away from me, I'd find you, Dee. God is my witness." He ate her lips, then kissed her. Hard. It tasted distinctly of warning. "Never run from me, understand? Run *to* me. I want to take care of you, but you have to let me in."

As if seeking to drive out the dark shadows of her past, he possessed her with a sudden rapid thrust, then another and another, each gaining force until she thought he might break her.

And then he did. He broke her with promises of faith and trust and love between hot murmurings of lust. He made her say again and again that she loved him more than any other and with each repetition he insisted she prove it with the relinquishing of her soul, her body, into his keep.

He kept them well, moving her however he liked, telling her to taste and touch him, and murmuring his satisfaction. When he said it was so very right that a woman should know her mate completely and feel the power her touch held over him, she felt unspeakable pleasure and blinding joy. Each touch, each kiss, was a vow, he continued, binding vows that could never be broken. Then he was demanding that she come, yes, come, Dee, to him, only to him. She did, again and again, while he refused himself the same release.

"No more," she whimpered weakly. She couldn't think, couldn't even lift an arm. "Matthew, no more."

"Yes, more. Roll over, wife."

Wife? He must have said *night,* she decided, dazed.

"Can't move? Let me help." He gently turned her onto her stomach.

Cool air brushed over her fevered, damp skin. Then he was kissing her back, his lips tracing her spine and lulling her exhausted body into the sweetest oblivion. She was almost asleep when he tucked her in.

"Still with me?" he whispered. She mumbled a groggy assent. "Good, because I've got something to say that you need to remember. I've been patient, but my patience goes only so far." He stroked the tangled hair from her face and pressed a tender kiss to her temple. "Sleep on that, Dee. But don't take too long to wake up to the kind of man you're in so deep with, you'd never get away from him."

Was she dreaming, imagining the edge of caution in his tone? "Ever . . . get . . . away?" she repeated.

"Don't even try, ever. I can outrun you. I can outwait you. But a day will come when I won't wait anymore. When it does, don't try to deceive me because I'll wear you down until you drop. And that, Dee, is a vow you'd be wise to heed." The mattress shifted beneath her as he stood up. She reached for him and felt only emptiness. "Merry Christmas. And God bless you, my wife."

That word again. *Night,* he must have said *good night.* "Merry Christmas," she whispered against the pillow that should have been his chest. She heard what might have been the clicking of her doorlock or the cocking of a pistol. Was it Vince or Nick or a paid henchman?

And then she was in the realm of dreams and she was running, running down an empty street until she stumbled and fell. The sound of quick footsteps filled her ears while white mist swirled around her in the darkness.

On her hands and knees she turned in slow motion. A scream of terror lodged in her throat.

The mist parted and darkness became radiant light. Matthew loomed tall above her. He extended his hand, but hers were stuck in the ground and she couldn't grasp what she was desperate to take.

He spoke. "You're mine now. I'll take care of you. Don't ever run from me again. Run to—"

She heard the whirr of a bullet before it struck. Matthew looked at her so strangely, more shock than pain etched into his features. An angel was bleeding rivulets of red down his bare chest.

The hand he'd extended became a charred wing. Her own hands were suddenly free, and she reached up to grasp him, but he was gone.

She looked to heaven to plead, to curse and pray, and above her she saw him ascending, rising through the air.

He shook his head as he blew her a departing kiss. "Why didn't you take my hand? Why didn't you trust me? You were mine. Always mine. You should have run to me."

"Matthew," she screamed. "Don't leave me. Dear God, please don't leave—"

"Run to me, Dee. Only . . . *to* . . . *me*."

Fifteen

As Valentine's Day approached, Matt had more on his mind than which box of candy to select or flowers to send. Tapping a pen against the church ledger, he battled the same old frustration.

What was he doing wrong? Hadn't he established his place in Dee's life? Had he not repeatedly assured her by his actions and words that between them and God no problem was insurmountable?

The temptation to quiz Jason and Loren was great. Did they believe she was their mother, as he had? If so, he couldn't risk destroying their belief.

But no matter how just Dee's cause was, she was guilty of kidnapping. A severe criminal offense. His refusal to report it was a crime in itself.

Matthew rubbed his forehead and felt the creases that seemed grooved there. His monthly trip to the homeless shelter was coming up, and he didn't want to leave Dee alone. But this time he was going to make some careful inquiries through certain trustworthy connections.

His position at the shelter had grown considerably during his previous association with it. He'd belonged to a network of top-notch lawyers, judges, congressmen, even the governor. They'd consulted with him on the issue of the homeless, and he'd even counseled the governor on other problems. Even state officials had personal difficulties and needed the ear of someone they could trust to keep the matter confidential.

Yep, him and the governor were on a first-name basis. The governor was still in office, even if Matthew Peters, the tireless worker, had worn out.

But he couldn't call in favors without Dee's cooperation. His one mention of having friends in authority had met with an abrupt good-night.

Giving up on getting any work done, Matthew slammed the ledger shut. Just as he grabbed his coat, he heard a soft knock at the open door and turned to see Dee walk in.

"Got a minute, Reverend?" She wiped moist palms over her skirt, hoping he wouldn't detect her nervousness.

"For you? I've got all the time in the world." He tossed aside his coat and kicked the door shut. "It's not often I see you so early on a weekday. Is anything wrong?"

"No," she said quickly, hoping he wouldn't detect that it was a lie. "I was just missing you and decided I could use a kiss."

His familiar touch to her cheek somewhat calmed her fears.

"So you wanna neck, huh? Then welcome to my private chambers and let's get this counseling session under way."

They were kissing like mad when the door banged open. Dee didn't comprehend that they were no longer alone until she heard Sally Henderson gasp out, "*My God.* Oh . . . my . . . *God!*"

"You should have knocked, Sally." Matthew had pulled away from Dee and was now staring at Mrs. Henderson.

"I did knock, *Rev.* Peters. Apparently the two of you were too busy to notice." Her eyes narrowed to mean little slits. "I'll make sure that the church hears about this. For shame. You, a man of God, with this cheap woman."

"Shut your mouth. This woman is not cheap—she's going to be my wife. Take that to the rest of the church."

"Matthew, no! We *can't* get married. Please, Matthew, don't say anything that I can't honor."

"Well, well, Reverend, there seems to be a difference of opinion. You should have told *her*, not me, to keep the trap shut. Now, if you'll excuse me, I have some important phone calls to make regarding a minister who's not fit to wear the robes the *ex*-church pianist has likely touched in the most unseemly places. May I suggest that you turn the lock before picking up where you left off when I interrupted?"

Absolute silence followed Sally's departure. Matt ground his teeth while Dee took in shallow breaths. She wanted to touch him, beg his understanding. She wanted to turn back the clock—

Matthew hit the wall with a fist. "You amaze me, Dee. Absolutely amaze me. For being so concerned about my reputation, you did a hell of a job to help ruin it. Why didn't you back me up when I needed you most?"

"Because . . ." Because she loved him too much to compromise his safety, and this morning when she'd answered the phone, a man had said "Sorry, wrong number," then hung up, sending her borrowed security into a tailspin.

"Because, Matthew, being under fire from a hateful old biddy is no reason for us to get married. This time it's *my* standards I'm unwilling to compromise."

"We're meant to be married. We're *getting* married. And the reason you're trying to dodge it has nothing to do with the tripe you just gave me and everything to do with the lies you've fed me since the day we met."

"No," she whispered, edging to the door. Think, she ordered herself. She had to think of lies to cover her lies. And she had to get away before he wrung the truth from her. "We-we'll talk later," she stammered. "Not . . . not now."

"Later *is* now," he said softly as he walked toward her. When he reached her, she'd cracked open the door and he slammed his palm against it, closing it with a bang. She shrank back. "I warned you a day would come when my patience would snap. Do you hear the snap now? Out with it, Dee." And then he roared, "Out with it!"

"I won't talk to you like this," she said. The shaking in her voice matched the trembling of her body. "You're out of control, Matthew."

"Damn right I am. Game's up. Time's out. You're telling me who and what you're running from."

"I'm telling you to back off. I'm telling you that I'm deeply sorry for what happened and I won't come back to this church. Tell them I seduced you and you've repented. Maybe they'll give you another chance so you won't lose your second pastorship and make things worse with your father."

"My father is the least of my concerns at the moment. Another father, Vince, is uppermost in my mind. Who is he, *really*? What kind of man can keep you so scared?"

"His name is one you'll stay healthier by not knowing. I'm bad news, Reverend. If you're smart, you'll tell me we're through and—"

"And if you're trying to make me mad, lady, you're more than succeeding. I don't want a martyr. I want a wife and you're it. You've been it since we had carnal knowledge of each other. Remember that night? You lost your virginity."

She stared at him mutely and swayed with shock. Matt caught her by the arms.

"You knew. You *knew*. And said nothing."

"I said plenty, only you refused to listen. Think, Dee. How many times have I all but pleaded for you to let me help?"

She couldn't deny it. The signs of his knowledge had been there, but she'd kept silent anyway, rationalizing that as long as she did, the truth couldn't steal their happiness. Now the thief had come, and what they'd had was slipping away too fast.

"Then you realize that my life is a sham. A lie."

"It's no way to live, Dee." His grip loosened, and as he stroked her arms, she could feel him willing his strength to her. "Do you actually think I would violate your trust after I washed your blood from my hands, my coat?"

At that moment she damned the most cherished night of her existence. She damned the virtue she'd rejoiced in giving only to him. And she damned her own weakness that made her almost glad it had happened. Perhaps now she *could* share her burden with Matthew and bear it alone no more.

She took a steadying breath. "Your hands aren't the only ones that have had blood on them. Vince was my brother-in-law. When my sister, Alexis, wanted to divorce him and gain custody of the kids, he killed her. But I can't prove it."

"Murdered for wanting a divorce? That's crazy."

"Not as crazy as my going to the police with no evidence, only allegations against a prominent citizen whose casinos bring a lot of money into the state."

"There must be something or someone who could back you up."

"I didn't try to find out. You see, word about what I'd done got leaked to Vince right away, and he told me that I could make sure my parents stayed healthy by keeping quiet. He was very persuasive." She laughed, but the sound was brittle.

"How did Alexis die?" Matthew asked softly.

"They said she lost control of her car while she was driving and crashed. I didn't believe it then, and I still don't. Alexis was a very careful driver. Vince—or someone he'd paid—had to have tampered with the car. You see, the men in his family have an unnatural need to keep what they claim is theirs. I found that out for myself."

He shook his head. "How?"

"Nick is Vince's brother. We were engaged. He proposed when he was just out of law school, and I was home for the summer after my first year at Juiliard.

"Juiliard. Impressive. And as much as I hate to say it, so is a man willing to wait for a woman. You never slept with him."

"Nick had plenty of women, I found out later. He wanted a virgin on his wedding night, and he was delighted it was a requirement I could fulfill." She paused. "Nick was obsessed with me."

"Obsessed with you?" he repeated, his face filled with incredulity.

Dee nodded. "He has a sick need to own, to have control over what he thinks he loves. It was as if *my* body were his. As if I were a prize, an item in a store window he admired."

"That's twisted, Dee."

"Yes," she said distantly. "Anyway, a month before the wedding Alexis swore me to silence, then let me know that Vince and Nick were involved with some rough people. She did what she could to save me from getting trapped, as she was."

Dee shook her head at the biting memory. "I didn't want to believe it, Matt. But my trust was shaken and I wanted to call off the marriage. That's when I found out what kind of man Nick really was. He slapped me and said if I didn't go through with the wedding, he'd make me regret it."

Matt looked ready to do bodily harm to Nick. "And did he?"

"In spades. If he couldn't have me, no one would. He kept me under constant surveillance— even after I left for another state. I dated one man twice before he was mysteriously beaten up. When I realized there was no escaping him, I moved back to Vegas. That was three years ago. Alexis's marriage had gone from bad to horrible, and the kids spent a lot of time with me. I think Vince was indulging their need for a mother after she died. But since he'd found out that I had gone to the police, I knew he'd eventually get rid of me too."

"And so you ran away with the kids."

"Not for a while. It wasn't easy, but I managed to get copies of their school and shot records when I picked them up the last day of class. By then I was friendly with the man keeping tabs on us. He finally joined me for a drink one night in August."

"Spiked it, did you?" Matt smiled, and she warmed to his pride in her desperate act.

"Let's just say by the time he woke up, we were gone. I told the kids we were taking a walk. I got them ice cream cones and I bought a fern. All the while I kept looking over my shoulder." The memory of that plant's role in their first meeting coaxed an ironic chuckle from Matthew and a painful sigh from her.

"I can just see it, Dee. A woman shopping with two children eating ice cream. Perfect. Perfectly innocent."

"That was the general idea. Once I was confident we weren't being followed, I took them to where I'd parked the car I bought with cash. I left everything I owned behind, except for a few clothes I stashed at the last minute in a big purse. I made several car trades before we ended up here in Hayes."

"*Incredible*," he breathed. "How much do the kids know?"

"Enough to keep quiet and pretend I'm their mom. Which isn't hard. I can still hear them crying to me for help every time they saw their father slap Alexis around. They are my children, Matthew, and I'd kill before giving them back. We're a family, and we're bound by more than blood. We share loyalties. We share shame. We shared you."

"You still share me. You always will."

Didn't he get it? Didn't he grasp where all this was leading? But no, his voice was calm and his face expressed some odd expectation.

"The children and I share other things too, Matt. Protection. I'm doing my best to protect them from being sucked into their father's world. Vince won't get them as long as I'm around."

"Not as long as I'm around either . . . and that's going to be for the rest of our lives." Matthew grasped her shoulders. His gaze was tender, as was his smile, but what she wanted was his wrath. Anything except this gentle touch that made her long to embrace his hope.

"I knew the first day we met, there was something special inside you, though I had no idea you were so courageous." His words were an intimate murmur. "I hope you like the ring I picked out. The only thing that has kept it off your finger is the trust you've just given me."

She thought she was going to be sick. When she covered her mouth, he winked, obviously mistaking the cause.

"Surely, you're not surprised that I'm proposing

for the second time in an hour. After all, your first refusal doesn't count since the reason you refused is gone."

He released her and pulled out a desk drawer. And then he was holding out an open heart-shaped white velvet box. A simple gold and diamond ring winked up at her. Dee's mouth worked, but no words would come. Oh, this seemed cruel, crueler than any punishment Nick or Vince could devise.

"Shut the box," she whispered sharply. "Didn't you hear me? Shut it! Put it away. Get it away from me, now. Now!"

She clutched at her heart, which was breaking apart like shattered glass. The way he was looking at her, stunned and then hurt—oh, dear Lord, she couldn't bear it.

"I guess I can take that as a second no." He closed the box and slammed it down on the desk, then threw up his hands. "What the hell is it now? You've told me everything. Nothing's between us any more but this damnable refusal of yours to accept what's meant to be."

"Nothing between us but that?" she cried in disbelief. "Matt, it's a lost cause, don't you see? The problem hasn't gone away. There's no future for us." Dee gripped his arms and tried to shake him out of his maddening stillness. He was immovable.

"Where is your faith, woman?" he said quietly. "If not in heaven, then in me. How many times have I vowed to you my protection? My love? Do you believe in me so little that you would spit on what I'm offering you?"

Tears slid down her cheeks. She wiped them, praying for a strength to counter his.

"Your love means everything to me, Matt, but you have to realize that I'm living on borrowed time. Your protection I covet, but it can't compete with this thing that won't stop until I'm found. It could be soon."

"What makes you think so?"

"The reason I came here today. A man had just called and said 'wrong number,' then hung up. Maybe it was, maybe it wasn't, but we can't live our lives wondering how much time we have left each time the phone rings."

"But we won't live that way because we're making a call of our own." He reached for the phone.

"Who are you calling?" she demanded.

"The authorities, Dee. I have friends who can intercede."

"No! You don't know who you're dealing with or you wouldn't even suggest something so stupid."

"What's stupid is being a sitting duck."

"Maybe so, Matt, but better sitting than napping in the bottom of a casket." She put her hand down over his. "I forbid you to call anyone you know, no matter who they are."

"I say it's time we bring in some honest officials who have a stake in justice, not casinos."

"Okay, go ahead," she said haltingly. "But before you hang up, the house across the street will be vacant."

"Is that a threat?"

"A promise. Unless you can meet my terms."

"Your terms?" he repeated caustically. "I suppose that means you want an affair, not marriage? Maybe settle for a few stolen fornications until you get nervous and run again?"

"Yes," she said in a rush. "Yes, exactly. Tell your church that I tempted you and you fell. With luck and a prayer you can stay employed here. Without it, you have the homeless shelter to go back to. You couldn't see me often either way, but, Matthew, it is something."

"So I can live in my parsonage or hundreds of

miles away, but never share a home with you." He stared at her hard. "That's something, all right."

She gripped his robe. "But you can visit. Late at night, once the neighbors are asleep. We'll give every appearance of having cut our ties. Then, if questions are asked, the answer will be that we're no longer involved. If I have to leave fast, I'll get in touch once it's safe. Okay? Say it's okay. Please, Matthew. I'm begging you."

Her voice was moving, pitiful. His sympathy ran deep even while his anger and determination escalated. Poor Dee, he thought, that you could believe I would debase us to this. How much you still have to learn about me.

"So," he said slowly, "the honeymoon's over. If I want to be in your life, I settle for less than what we both deserve and go along with the farce. Some choice, Dee." He drew his hand from the phone.

"Then you won't call your people?"

"Looks like your call cancels mine. Can I come over tonight after the kids are in bed? Or does that violate your standards of subterfuge?"

She winced but didn't back down. "Don't. Give it one month from today—at midnight."

"And if I don't abide by your rules?"

Dee hugged herself close to keep from coming apart. "Then I'm gone and we're finished."

He held her gaze as he reached for the door, stretching out the taut moment until he was certain she realized the potential consequences of her ultimatum.

Then he turned the lock and walked slowly back to his desk. In one abrupt movement he slid papers, the phone, the engagement ring to the floor.

"In that case, lover, the affair's in full swing and I want something to dream about for the next month. Happy, Dee?"

Though her eyes shimmered with hurt, he was compelled to drive home a crucial point.

"Matthew, please. *Please.* Don't reduce us to this."

"I didn't reduce us. You did." When he motioned her to the desk, she stiffly obeyed. "What's wrong? Why aren't you taking off your panties for the gigolo? Time's short, and that's something we have precious little of," he said as he pulled out a foil packet from his wallet.

"Why are you being so horrid, Matthew?"

"Weren't these your terms for our relationship?" He scratched his head, pretending to look confused. "Did I misunderstand somehow? Had you meant that you'll marry me and let me handle the problem, trust me enough to see this through with you? No?" The sound he made smacked of distaste. "Okay, I'm easy. We'll switch roles. Instead of me being your boy-toy, spread your legs and be my mistress. Unless you've got the guts to put that ring on your finger and be my wife."

She was crying, her hands shaking badly as she took off her jeans and panties, then laid half clothed upon the desk.

"You're not enjoying this," he said quietly. He couldn't see her face because both of her hands were covering it. "Look at me," he demanded, jerking them away. "Why aren't you enjoying this?"

"How can I?" she said in such agony that he cringed inside. "This isn't us. This isn't who we are."

"It *wasn't* what we were until you gave us no alternative. I've had affairs, several, in fact, even if you haven't. This is it, Dee. This is what you insist we be for as long as we can steal it. Great, isn't it? Don't you love getting nailed by a man who knows all the right buttons to hit? C'mon, babe, let's get it on. We're on a stopwatch, not a lifetime or eternity together."

"I hate this," she sobbed.

"But you don't hate me." He kissed her softly, achingly sweetly, priming her for a swift seduction. "You love me."

"Yes. More than my own life, I do love you."

"And because you do, you'll give me what I need—to be inside you before we say good-bye." He let the possible nightmare of parting forever linger before taking her.

He bathed her face with hungry kisses, tasting salty tears. "If this is all we can have, let's take it while we can. You said a month without this, without so much as a single 'I love you' or a shared confidence. You got your way, and that means we can never know which meeting will be our last. Should this be it, let's make it count."

Her arms went around his neck; her legs gripped him tightly and she sobbed against his shoulder. Matthew hid the grim set of his lips at the base of her throat.

There was an urgency to their lovemaking that had never been there before. The caresses they shared were fevered and demanding, as if each touch, each open-mouthed kiss, might be their last.

There was only the sound of labored breathing, the faint creak of the desk. They smelled of sweat, of lovers in heat. Each stroke he gave and she greedily took was a bonding. As he cradled her head and shielded her back from the hardness of wood, her cry of ecstasy emerged as a desperate sob.

And while he drank it from her lips, he pushed against her womb. And came. In silence he came while he stared down at this woman who he had claimed as wife.

"There now," he murmured, stroking wet hair from her temples. "Cry, just cry it all out. Let me hold you until you can't cry anymore and then . . . then I'll let you go."

His last few words only made her cry harder. It took a while for her tears to run dry.

Matthew dressed her while he whispered words of comfort and patience. But he was far from feeling patient. There was much work to be done, and the sooner Dee left, the sooner he could get to it.

"Ready?" he asked, rocking her in the cradle of his arms. He kissed her, then released her and walked to the door.

Matthew had to admire the courage evident in Dee's straight posture as she walked out of the office. She turned once, and raised her hand in farewell. He answered with a curt nod. Then she was gone.

Matthew shut the door and locked it. Reaching for the phone, he said a prayer before placing his call. All was silent in the church as he dialed.

But silent he would be no more.

Sixteen

"No, Trudy, not like that," Dee said sharply to her last student for the day. "Like this."

"I'm sorry, Ms. Sampson," the little girl whined. "Please don't be mad at me. I practiced, really I did."

What is wrong with you, Dee, scolding poor Trudy even more than you did the others? Keep this up and you will have to move, because you won't have a single pupil left and you've already lost five since Mrs. Busybody got busy and blabbed.

"I know you did, Trudy. And I shouldn't be so impatient. We'll skip the cadences today and work on your recital piece."

As Trudy proceeded to butcher Beethoven's *Für Elise*, Dee fought the urge to cover her ears and scream. Each wrong note rattled her frayed emotions.

She couldn't go on like this or she'd lose what little sanity she had left. Three weeks and a day had passed. Three weeks and a day of pure hell without a single glimpse of Matthew.

He'd taken a leave from the church to search for guidance, Mrs. Adams had said when she came for the rent. She'd kindly added that Matthew had spoken his heart in his parting address. He'd apologized for offending some members' moral fiber, but it wasn't in him to lie and say he was sorry for loving a woman and physically professing that love.

He had also confessed to misleading the congregation he'd been honored to serve, and explained the background that he'd omitted to mention before they welcomed him into their midst. The church, according to Mrs. Adams, had been very moved by his honesty and courage and insisted that he stay at the parsonage. Most missed him greatly. As for the colleague Matt asked the hiring board to give a try, the man was made of lesser stuff. He couldn't compete with Matthew's gift of delivering a meaningful sermon. And his interest in the needy was nonexistent.

It had taken Dee all of two weeks to realize that no one and nothing, including her fears, could compete with Matthew. He'd taught her a harsh yet loving lesson—only it hadn't sunk in until he was nowhere to be found.

Damn you, Matthew, damn you for leaving no matter what I said. I take back the month. Make it three weeks, make it today. . . .

"Ms. Sampson? Ms. Sampson, did I do okay?"

Dee blinked, trying to focus on the little girl who had stopped playing.

"Yes, Trudy," she said. "Very good." Reaching for a small tin on top of the piano, Dee picked out two star-shaped stickers and put them on the music sheet. "There you go, an extra one for effort. Keep up the fine work and I'll see you next week."

Once Trudy was out the door, Dee went to her bedroom.

Her hand hovered over the phone. Matthew

should be at the homeless shelter today. If she got through to him there, what would she say?

Maybe she should tell him that she was a wreck who'd rather trust his promises of protection than live alone with constant fear. Or she could play on his soft spot for two confused kids who were demanding answers. Why was Rev. Matthew gone? And why didn't God listen to their prayers and bring him back? It was her fault, and if they found out, they might never forgive her for taking away the best dad they'd ever had.

Dee took several deep breaths before lifting the receiver. She punched the number to the homeless shelter office.

He wasn't there. They expected him today, but he hadn't arrived. Could they take a message, since he'd surely be in no later than tomorrow? Yes, they'd tell him it was important and to call right away.

Dee frowned as she hung up. How strange for him to miss work; no one was more dependable than Matthew. She quickly phoned the parsonage. As she expected, she got an answering machine.

His voice rippled through her, his wonderful voice that brought all that had died inside her back to life.

Before she could leave a message, she was distracted by the sound of running feet and Loren and Jason's yelling.

"Dee! Dee! Where are you? *Dee!*"

"Here. For pity's sake, what's wrong?"

Jason almost ran her down before she caught his shoulders.

"A man," he panted. "Following us, in a car."

"Sweet heaven," she whispered. "You're certain of it?"

Loren nodded. "But we cut down an alley and

jumped some fences. He didn't see which house we went into. We made double sure."

Anxiety pumped through Dee. She couldn't seem to breathe. Why hadn't she listened to Matthew sooner? Had they already gotten to him? Was he hurt, or . . .

She couldn't think it or she'd be paralyzed.

Dee sent Jason and Loren from the room, then dialed the parsonage again and left a message for Matthew to pray for her soul. After hanging up, she lifted the end of her mattress. With cold, trembling hands, she pulled out the gun.

"Hear that, Reverend? She wants you to pray." Turning his attention from the parsonage answering machine, Vince laughed softly, then pointed the barrel of the pistol he held at Matthew. "Not a bad idea. You'd better pray she doesn't go to the police around here."

"I can handle the police, no problem." Nick drummed his fingers on a briefcase. "I've done my homework, gotten our legal contacts lined up. We can come down on Dee so hard no amount of praying will dig her out . . . unless you're feeling generous toward your brother?"

"We'll see."

Nick glared at Matthew, and Matthew fought the urge to cram his fist down the lawyer's throat. "So tell me, choirboy, how does she screw?"

"Like a virgin," he replied smoothly. "Thanks, Nicky. So thoughtful of you to ensure she was intact for me. Such a rare and memorable experience."

Nick lunged, but Vince caught him. "I'm suddenly feeling generous. Keep your cool and maybe instead of snuffing the bitch, I'll let you stash her at your place in Mexico."

"Over my dead body," Matthew said, his lips barely moving.

"We could arrange that easy," Vince said, chuckling. His smile was that of a gambler laying down the winning hand. "Just remember, do exactly what we tell you. One wrong move from you and Ms. Dee Sampson ends up in the morgue tonight."

Seventeen

As the sun went down and night approached, Dee turned on all the lights, shut all the curtains, and checked the locks yet again before sitting on the couch where Jason and Loren huddled.

"I'm scared, Dee, really scared." Loren gripped her hand, and Dee squeezed it in reassurance.

"We'll be all right. If Matthew doesn't call by tomorrow, we'll report him missing." The uncertainty of his whereabouts had made up her mind to stay instead of taking to the highway. If only she knew how to get in touch with the friends Matthew had mentioned in his office.

At nine o'clock she sent the children to her bedroom with instructions to dial 911 at the first sound of trouble. At precisely ten o'clock a sharp knock sounded at the front door. Dee reached under the couch and clasped the gun in a hand so sweaty she feared the weapon might slide from her grip. For that reason she slid the gun into a pocket concealed by the generous folds of her peasant skirt.

"Who is it?" she demanded.

"Dee, it's Matthew. Open up."

"Matthew!" Dee flung the door open, but he stepped back from her outstretched hands. His eyes sent warning signals at the same time they relayed hunger for the sight of her.

"Got your message." His words were clipped. "Can I come in so we can talk?"

"Certainly." Her gaze darted outside, but she saw nothing unusual.

Matthew brushed past her, and she heard him say under his breath, "Act normal and do what I say."

He pressed her against the entry wall and kissed her. Dee felt his hand reach out and flick off the lights for the porch and entry. Why did he do that, she wondered as desire mixed with her rising apprehension.

Her ears picked up the sound of footsteps on the porch. Her senses went wild, and she could smell her own fear.

"Nice job, Reverend." It was Nick's voice. Bile was in Dee's throat as Matthew pulled away from her. The front door closed and the entry light came on. She saw Nick and Vince standing inside her house, smiling, their white teeth flashing in predatory grins. Then Vince was rushing past her. She wanted to stop him, but Nick was suddenly tracing her jaw with the cool metal of the silencer fitted on his revolver.

"How are you doing, Dee? Like a mental case, I missed you." She didn't give him the satisfaction of flinching. "Do me a favor? Be smart. I'd rather not visit you in the state pen or send flowers to your wake."

"And I'd rather rot behind bars or fertilize the ground than pick up where I left off with you."

Nick raised a brow. "If you give me a second chance, I could change your mind."

Dee looked at Matthew, filling herself with the

sight of him, knowing she would agree to anything to protect him. "I suppose it's possible," she said, nearly gagging on the words. "Let him go and I'll see what I can do about getting over my grudge."

"Save the reunion, Nick," she heard Vince say behind her back. She whirled around and saw him clutching Jason with one arm, Loren with the other. The children turned wide, pleading eyes from her to Matthew. "Our driver is idling behind the house, and my kids are ready for a nice, quiet trip home. We even have sodas and everything they could want for the plane ride. We're going to have fun, right, kids?"

He sounded for all the world like a loving father, and Nick was smiling like an indulgent uncle.

"You won't hurt Rev. Matt, will you, Dad?" Jason asked. "Me and Loren, we'll be really good. We won't run away again so Aunt Dee won't have to come look for us. That's what happened, Dad. Honest. She got real mad at us and was going to bring us home, only we said if she tried, we'd run away where she couldn't find us."

"That's my boy," Vince said with pride. "Chip off the old block. You think fast on your feet. And just like I've taught you, you protect what's yours."

"But Rev. Matt—"

"Is staying behind, son. You see, he and your aunt had a falling out and won't be seeing each other again. But because he cares for you all so much, he's going to explain to your teachers and neighbors that your father was missing you and Aunt Dee decided it would be best to bring you back to your family. It was a sudden decision." The smile he flashed Matthew was chilling. "Right, Rev. Matt?"

"Right. How about a hug, kids, before you go? I'm sure going to miss you guys." He grasped Dee's arm and pulled her to him, while Jason and Loren rushed forward. The four of them gathered together tightly, a family being torn apart.

"Hurry it up," Vince snapped. "Our driver's waiting and we've already taken too long."

The lights went out. Dee felt Matthew shove them all to the floor, his weight on top of her.

"What the hell!" Vince shouted. "Nick, grab her. I'll get the kids. Jason! Loren! Where are you? Come back to your father, we have to get out. *Now!*"

Shouts of "This way!" were coming from the back, and footsteps were running up the porch. Just as the front door crashed against the wall, Dee twisted beneath Matthew, trying to reach for her pistol.

Suddenly there was light. Dee blinked up at Matthew's face and saw his face flood with relief. But then she felt him stiffen. The cock of a trigger sounded at the base of his skull.

"Nobody moves, understand?" Nick's voice was shaky. "Put down your guns, gentlemen, nice and easy. Good, very good. Vince, are you okay?"

"Yeah," Vince answered. Dee turned her head and saw that he was holding ten men at gunpoint, their weapons in a pile at his feet.

"Jason, Loren, get up and go stand by your dad." Once they'd obeyed, crying again and again, "Don't shoot him, Uncle Nick, please don't shoot him," Nick booted Matt in the side, and Dee felt the pain as if she took the cruel kick herself. She inched her hand to her thigh.

"On your feet, Reverend, or you're getting a one-way ticket to heaven."

"Suits me," Matthew said steadily. "Go ahead and shoot. I'm not afraid to die."

"No," Dee cried out. "Do what he says."

"Do what the man says, Rev. Peters," one of the men ordered. "No need for killing around here. Better yet, why don't we strike a deal?"

"Keep your stinking deals," Vince growled. "C'mon, Nick, forget her. Let's go!"

"Get up," Nick barked at Matthew. "The lady's got a date with an old friend who's through waiting."

The lady found her gun and fired.

Epilogue

The scent of gardenias and carnations and roses filled the church, while Sally Henderson, who'd arranged the flowers as a way of making amends, played Pachelbel's Canon in D on the piano. Rev. Carlton Peters stood in front of the pulpit.

Dee, waiting at the back of the church with her father, saw that every pew was filled. She watched as Loren walked down the aisle, past friends and neighbors and family. Even the governor was there, sitting with men and women dressed in leather jackets. When it was time to follow Loren, Dee silently thanked each person as she passed them.

She thanked the governor for bringing in the FBI. She thanked the agent who had acted as substitute minister and had slipped into her house one day and filled it with bugs. Two weeks after she had wounded Nick in the foot and he and Vince had been taken away, witnesses had been found who would testify as to what had been done to Alexis's car and who the order had come from.

When Dee and her father reached the pulpit, she released his arm, remembering the tearful reunion with her parents. Matthew had given her that, an even better present than his finding Cristofori and bringing it to the parsonage.

Smiling, Matthew stole a glance at his best man, Jason, before extending his hand to his bride. He pressed his lips to her palm and knew the wonder of a promise fulfilled. A miracle. Well, actually several miracles, including his dad waving the white flag once he'd learned his wayward son had almost ended up at the Pearly Gates.

Thanks, Father, he prayed silently. *As always, You came through.*

A few minutes later Matthew was saying, "I do," then drawing back his bride's veil and kissing her. Once Dee had told him they had no future together, but now he knew they had plenty of tomorrows.

The reception was held in the church basement, and after a couple of hours it was time for Dee and Matthew to leave. Cheers of good wishes followed them as they headed outside, where they were showered with birdseed. Laughing, they ran to the church van, which sported a Just Married sign on the rear window and trailed fifty cans from the rear bumper.

"What's in this?" Dee asked. After she'd climbed in, she'd thrown her bag to the backseat and noticed a cooler sitting on the floor.

"Your wedding gift, what else? A ten-pound bag of ice for our honeymoon night."

"Rev. Peters, are you sure this doesn't qualify as a sin?"

"If it does, so be it, beloved." He brought her hand to his lips and kissed the diamond-studded ring.

As he did, he thought he heard a benevolent chuckle from above and a voice blessing them with a whispered "Amen."

THE EDITOR'S CORNER

There's a lot to look forward to from LOVESWEPT in October—five fabulous stories from your favorites, and a delightful novel from an exciting new author. You know you can always rely on LOVESWEPT to provide six top-notch—and thrilling—romances each and every month.

Leading the lineup is Marcia Evanick, with **SWEET TEMPTATION,** LOVESWEPT #570. And sweet temptation is just what Augusta Bodine is, as Garrison Fisher soon finds out. Paleontologist Garrison thinks the Georgia peach can't survive roughing it in his dusty dinosaur-fossil dig—but she meets his skepticism with bewitching stubbornness and a wildfire taste for adventure that he quickly longs to explore . . . and satisfy. Marcia is at her best with this heartwarming and funny romance.

Strange occurrences and the magic of love are waiting for you on board the **SCARLET BUTTERFLY,** LOVESWEPT #571, by Sandra Chastain. Ever since Sean Rogan restored the ancient—and possibly haunted—ship, he'd been prepared for anything, except the woman he finds sleeping in his bunk! The rogue sea captain warns Carolina Evans that he's no safe haven in a storm, but she's intent on fulfilling a promise made long ago, a promise of love. Boldly imaginative, richly emotional, **SCARLET BUTTERFLY** is a winner from Sandra.

Please give a big welcome to new author Leanne Banks and her very first LOVESWEPT, **GUARDIAN ANGEL,** #572. In this enchanting romance Talia McKenzie is caught in the impossible situation of working very closely with Trace Barringer on a charity drive. He'd starred in her teenage daydreams, but now there's bad blood between their families. What is she to do, especially when Trace wants nothing less from her than her love? The answer makes for one surefire treat. Enjoy one of our New Faces of 1992!

Ever-popular Fayrene Preston creates a blazing inferno of desire in **IN THE HEAT OF THE NIGHT,** LOVESWEPT #573. Philip Killane expects trouble when Jacey finally comes home after so many years, for he's never forgotten the night she'd branded him with her fire, the night that had nearly ruined their lives. But he isn't prepared for the fact that his stepsister is more gorgeous than ever . . . or that he wants a second chance. An utterly sensational romance, with passion at its most potent—only from Fayrene!

In Gail Douglas's new LOVESWEPT, **THE LADY IS A SCAMP,** #574, the lady in the title is event planner Victoria Chase. She's usually poised and elegant, but businessman Dan Stewart upsets her equilibrium. Maybe it's his handshake that sets her on fire, or the intense blue eyes that see right inside her soul. She should be running to the hills instead of straight into his arms. This story showcases the winning charm of Gail's writing—plus a puppet and a clown who show our hero and heroine the path to love.

We end the month with **FORBIDDEN DREAMS** by Judy Gill, LOVESWEPT #575. When Jason O'Keefe blows back into Shell Landry's life with all the force of the winter storm howling outside her isolated cabin, they become trapped together in a cocoon of pleasure. Jason needs her to expose a con artist, and he also needs her kisses. Shell wants to trust him, but so much is at stake, including the secret that had finally brought her peace. Judy will leave you breathless with the elemental force raging between these two people.

On sale this month from FANFARE are three exciting novels. In **DAWN ON A JADE SEA** Jessica Bryan, the award-winning author of **ACROSS A WINE-DARK SEA,** once more intertwines romance, fantasy, and ancient history to create an utterly spellbinding story. Set against the stunning pageantry of ancient China, **DAWN ON A JADE SEA** brings together Rhea, a merperson from an undersea world, and Red Tiger, a son of merchants who has vowed revenge against the powerful nobleman who destroyed his family.

Now's your chance to grab a copy of **BLAZE,** by bestselling author Susan Johnson, and read the novel that won the *Romantic Times* award for Best Sensual Historical Romance and a Golden Certificate from *Affaire de Coeur* "for the quality, excellence of writing, entertainment and enjoyment it gave the readers." In this sizzling novel a Boston heiress is swept into a storm of passion she's never imagined, held spellbound by an Absarokee Indian who knows every woman's desires. . . .

Anytime we publish a book by Iris Johansen, it's an event—and **LAST BRIDGE HOME** shows why. Original, emotional, and sensual, it's romantic suspense at its most compelling. It begins with Jon Sandell, a man with many secrets and one remarkable power, appearing at Elizabeth Ramsey's cottage. When he reveals that he's there to protect her from danger, Elizabeth doesn't know whether this mesmerizing stranger is friend or foe. . . .

Also on sale this month in the Doubleday hardcover edition is **LADY DEFIANT** by Suzanne Robinson, a thrilling historical romance that brings back Blade, who was introduced in **LADY GALLANT.** Now Blade is one of Queen Elizabeth's most dangerous spies, and he must romance a beauty named Oriel who holds a clue that could alter the course of history.

Happy reading!

With warmest wishes,

Nita Taublib

Nita Taublib
Associate Publisher
LOVESWEPT and FANFARE

Don't miss these fabulous Bantam Fanfare
titles on sale in August.

DAWN ON A JADE SEA
by Jessica Bryan

BLAZE
by Susan Johnson

LAST BRIDGE HOME
by Iris Johansen

And in hardcover from Doubleday,
LADY DEFIANT
by Suzanne Robinson

DAWN ON A JADE SEA

by the award-winning author of
ACROSS A WINE-DARK SEA,

Jessica Bryan

*She was a shimmering beauty from a kingdom of legend. A
vision had brought Rhea to the glorious city of Ch'ang-an,
compelling her to seek a green-eyed, auburn-haired foreign
warrior called Zhao, the Red Tiger. Amid the jasmine of the
Imperial Garden, passion will be born, hot as fire, strong as
steel, eternal as the ocean tides . . .*

A.D. 829.

The storm struck at midnight.

Nothing was spared. Not the tiny villages nestled along the
coast, not the half-dozen fishing boats caught away from land,
and not the caravan of the merchant who at sunset had ordered
his men to camp beyond the hills that bordered the beach in an
effort to avoid the worst of the storm.

As each man struggled through the frenzied night, one
sound battered at his ears, making itself heard even over the
mad tumult of wind and rain and thunder.

The sea.

Leading a sleepy-eyed horse through the early dawn, Zhao
toiled along the last of the hills that overlooked the sea. Their
progress had been slow, for the path along the low cliffs was
narrow and rocky. The horse, its packs half-full with firewood
scavenged in the aftermath of the storm, had to pick its way
with care.

Suddenly the horse flung up his head, yet its gaze was not
fixed on Zhao, but on the beach. The beast's ears swiveled
nervously, his nostrils flared, then he shied and let out a
resounding snort of alarm. Zhao froze. At the same moment
that the horse had been frightened, something had called to

him. Gripping the lead rope tightly in one hand, he used the other to soothe the animal as he stared across the sand.

The beach wound like a broad golden ribbon between the gray and green cliffs and the shimmering blue waters of the sea. Driftwood and debris from the storm lay scattered across it, as though thrown there by giant hands. Zhao saw nothing else, though the presence still called to him. He told himself it was only his imagination and was turning away when a soft sound, the merest whisper, came to him on the wind. The horse whinnied sharply, jerking his head so hard, the boy had to use both hands on the rope to prevent the beast from bolting.

Following the animal's gaze, he saw what he had missed before. Between a large boulder and a pile of driftwood lay a naked woman, her body almost hidden by the twin bulks of rock and wood. At the moment his gaze lit upon her, rays of the still-red sun struck the woman's entire body, bathing it in a scarlet mist, as deep and luminous as rubies.

Involuntarily he gasped aloud. Stumbling in his haste, he hurried down to the beach. By the time he reached her, the angle of the sun had changed, and the woman lay in shadow. Tethering the horse to a sturdy driftwood log, the boy knelt beside her. She was so still, Zhao thought her dead. Then he caught the faintest flicker of an eyelid, and he let out a deep sigh. In the whole of his fifteen years he had never seen an unclothed woman. The sight of her transfixed him, so that for several moments all he could do was stare. She was more magnificent than any living creature he had ever seen.

Strands of seaweed had threaded themselves through the glorious mantle of midnight-black hair that lay in wild profusion around her shoulders. More of the dark-green seaweed was draped across her throat and breasts. Though still shocked, Zhao noted that while the body belonged to a ripe woman, the face—with its clearly non-Han features—was that of a girl barely twenty. He also saw that the entire naked length of her had been darkened by the sun in a most unseemly manner, the smooth unblemished skin gleaming bronze-gold in the strong light.

Only the merest rise and fall of the woman's chest and an occasional fluttering of blue-veined eyelids indicated the presence of life. Although she was silent now, he knew the moan had come from her.

Slowly he reached out for one of the woman's arms. A strange shiver went through Zhao as he tentatively laid his fingers upon her limp arm. The woman's flesh was unexpectedly warm, and, astonished at himself, he felt his heartbeat quicken.

He would not have believed the woman could become any more beautiful. But at the touch of his hand, her long black eye lashes quivered and her eyes opened. Gray eyes. As silvery deep and beyond fathoming as a sea in winter.

Stunned, Zhao stared into the depths of those misty, enigmatic eyes. Though the woman was a stranger to him, he'd swear he saw a glimmer of recognition in her gaze. In the instant before she closed her eyes again, he knew his world had forever changed.

Trembling, he released the flaccid wrist he had been holding. Splashes of reddish-brown stained the sand beneath the woman's head. Looking closer, he saw that a deep gash, nearly hidden in the dark mass of her hair, was seeping blood. He drew in his breath. The woman needed help, but to move her without knowing the extent of her hurts could be even worse than not to help her at all.

He clambered to his feet. Ignoring the horse's plaintive whinny, he dashed off down the beach, running as though wings had attached themselves to his heels.

The caravan of Zhao's grand-uncle and head of the clan was not far from where the injured woman lay. But by the time he saw the hide tents and kneeling camels in the distance, Zhao was gulping for air, his lungs burning as if he were breathing fire. To his horror neither his grand-uncle nor his father—the only two men in the caravan with any knowledge of healing— were in camp.

He would have to take his father's healing pouch and care for the woman himself, he thought as he raced toward the tent he shared with his father. Until his elder relatives returned, there was no one he could trust with the discovery of a dazed and naked woman on the beach. Moments later he emerged from the tent and tore out of camp.

When he finally caught sight of his tethered horse, Zhao heaved a gasping prayer that the woman would still be alive.

Loaded down with the heavy pouch as well as a piece of satin to wrap her in, he stumbled toward the spot where she lay.

It was empty.

Only the bloodstained patch of sand showed that she had been there at all. He stared wildly around him, up at the cliffs, then toward the water. He saw her there, tall and proud-breasted, like some being not of this earth, wading deliberately into the sea.

"Lady!" he screamed as he ran toward her.

She glanced at him, a brief turning of that raven-maned head. In the bright sunlight he caught a glimpse of her eyes, silvery and strangely bright, like polished mirrors in the fierce glitter of sun and water. Then she dived.

"No, Lady, no!"

Frantically he threw himself forward. His arms grasped only air, and with a jarring thud he fell facedown in the wet sand. Leaping to his feet, he dashed into the sea, his gaze desperately searching the rolling waves. He saw her. She was swimming, but in a manner Zhao had never seen, nor even imagined possible.

Arms pressed close to her sides so that she resembled a pale-brown dolphin, the woman was undulating across the sapphire waves. Her body cut through the water with a speed and power that caused Zhao's next shout to strangle in his throat.

"La-lady," he croaked, then stood there in silence, watching her disappear. Unexpectedly a lump rose into his throat, and an inexplicable pain stabbed his breast. All around him he suddenly felt the presence of things unseen and not understood, but longed for nonetheless. Filled with grief and a strange yearning, he stood for a long time, ankle-deep in the shifting waves, gazing out to sea.

BLAZE
by
Susan Johnson
author of FORBIDDEN and SINFUL

The gold rush sparked a new American dream for those who staked their claims in the rich soil of undeveloped Indian territories. To Blaze Braddock, beautiful, pampered daughter of a millionaire, it was a chance to flee the stifling codes of Boston society. But when Jon Hazard Black, a proud young Absarokee chief, challenged her father's land claim, Blaze was swept up in a storm of passions she had never before even imagined . . .

When the evening star appeared in the sky, after a quiet if heated discussion, Hazard tied Blaze to him in two places, at waist and wrist, then lay down on the narrow bed and, exhausted, slept through the night for the first time in five days.

Lying very still, Blaze listened to Hazard's even breathing, until the slow, easy rhythm seemed part of her own respiration, until the warmth of the large man pressed close to her stole into her senses with an inexplicable rush of pleasure she could neither control nor deny. Cautiously she turned her head a millimeter in his direction, waited, then, observing no change in the deep, resonant breathing, slowly eased her glance around until he was fully within her gaze.

It came over her suddenly, as it always did—his unbearable beauty, the magnificence muted now in sleep to mere splendor. She watched him while the fading pastels of twilight disappeared into the void of night. Watched the play of light over the stark cheekbones, visually traced the perfect symmetry of finely chiseled nose. His sculptured mouth was prominently sensual—no austerity there, she noted. No, definitely not austere. And only with effort did she restrain herself from outlining that sensuous mouth with her fingertips. Even his brows were like delicate winged creatures, dark silky creatures that whispered to be touched. Blaze clenched her fingers tightly against the overpowering urge. And when his thick lashes fluttered suddenly, she caught her breath, fearful the sharp black eyes might open and find her own gaze transfixed. But he only sighed lightly, his fingers unconsciously tightening on the braided rawhide coiled around his hand.

As she observed him, taking in the sight and sound, the sage-sweet scent so much a part of these mountains it clung to everything, she suddenly saw, through unclouded vision, a different Hazard Black. Not the sensual, seductive man, as she had seen him, not the ruthless killer, as others saw him, not even an "Indian from an alien culture." She saw only a man, seeming as vulnerable as a child in his sleep. A man, beautiful beyond words but, transcending his physical perfection, beautiful in spirit, imbued with an indomitable courage, fearless against overwhelming odds. Odds any practical man would have refused. Jon Hazard Black had set himself against one of the most powerful mining cartels in the world. And he intended to stand his ground.

But later, in the roil and tumult of chaotic half sleep and black dreams, her logic and emotion at war, she felt the return of her initial outrage and resentment at his monumental arrogance at taking her hostage. How dare he, she thought with renewed vigor. *How the hell dare he!*

"You can't keep me here!" he heard her hiss as the first light of dawn appeared. Grunting softly, he rolled over, still half asleep, and the braided leather rope binding them tightened. The movement brought her hard against his back. He vaguely heard a quiet gasp and felt her stiffen. Then silence. Blessed silence, he thought, recalling her volatile temper.

She repeated the phrase in a scathing whisper. He opened one eye briefly, casting a glance over his bare shoulder, and encountered snapping blue eyes. "Sorry," he murmured truthfully, for he knew already that his life had become endlessly complicated because of one Miss Venetia Braddock.

"Sorry? *You're* sorry?" she muttered incredulously. And then proceeded to read him the riot act until he exasperatedly answered in his own rush of temper, *"Enough!"*

But she wouldn't stop, the words tumbling out, furious and hot with defiance, like clubs beating and flailing at his head. He had to kiss her to arrest the torrent of abusive rage. A hand over her mouth might have worked as well, he admitted as his lips covered hers, but logic relinquished the field hastily to an unexplained desire to quiet her in a more pleasurable way.

She tasted sweet and welcoming, he thought, settling himself in an unconsciously fluid maneuver between her legs. How warm she was . . . and soft. Loosening the coiled rope from his hand, his fingers tangled in the silk of her hair, holding her like a precious gift, while his lips and tongue explored the luscious interior of her mouth.

He couldn't help himself. Didn't want to. She was here, his for the taking. And in a flashing second he realized how much he'd missed having a woman near. She felt like homecoming and rapture and soul-deep solace. When he raised his mouth the idyll was shattered.

"You . . . you . . . animal," she sputtered, her head turning fitfully in his grasp, her eyes glowering. "You odious, abominable—"

". . . savage," he finished softly and took her mouth again. This time in a hard, possessive invasion that put to use all the expertise acquired so pleasurably over the years. When he lifted his mouth a second time, long minutes later, his slow, sure skill had left her trembling and breathless. The sputter, modified, was now more like a sigh.

"This . . . will . . . never . . ."

". . . get any gold mined," Hazard whispered, a smile curling through the words. "You're right, *sweet bia* . . . and I'll try to get you into the kitchen very soon"—his smile widened—"so you can make me breakfast. Are you ready to begin earning your keep?" He tugged her closer with the rawhide still tied around her waist.

She didn't answer at first. Couldn't. Didn't want to. Didn't know her own mind. But his fingers slipped between her thighs and slid upward like devil's sorcery, very slowly at first, tantalizing, waiting for her to ask for more. And when she arched her hips in response, his slim fingers eased into her sweetness. She cried out and reached for him, her arms twining tightly around his neck.

He raised himself slightly against the pressure of her hands and, looking down at her exquisite, flushed face, asked again, "Are you ready to earn your keep?" His fingers continued to stroke languidly and she moaned softly with each delicate movement. Bending near, his lips hovered in a whisper above hers. "Say yes, little rich girl." His fingers drifted deeper and her nails dug into his shoulders. "Say you'll cook for me."

His obliging movements stopped and she quickly whispered, "Yes."

"And clean for me."

"Yes," she breathed.

"And do anything else."

"Oh—please, yes."

His fingers slid free and he moved over her gently.

"Now," she cried.

"Soon," he said and eased his body down.

The next half-formed plea died in a breathy moan as he glided, hard and long, into her urging womanly warmth. How could she, he thought with pleasure, feel so excruciatingly fine?

How could he, she thought, with a shameful thrill, arching against his spearing invasion, know I want him so?

An hour later, when the rawhide shackle had long since been untied by gentle fingers, and when Jon Hazard Black had given in to his hostage's demands as many times as any able man would, he kissed her one last time, rose from the shambles of the bed, and said, "I'm going to bathe in the stream behind the cabin. Would you care to join me?"

"Is it cold?"

"Brisk."

"I know mountain streams. No, thank you."

He smiled. "Suit yourself. Breakfast in ten minutes?"

"Is that an invitation?"

"Not exactly. Call it . . . a diplomatic request." He could see the stubborn set of her jaw begin to form. "*Very* diplomatic," he cajoled, reaching down to touch her pretty mouth with a placating finger. "Relax, Boston, I'm no ogre. I'll help."

"Then let me go," Blaze said in a hurried rushing breath, fearful of staying with him for reasons that had nothing at all to do with mining claims.

Hazard's half-lowered eyelids covered eyes so dark they were unreadable. "I wish I could," he said quietly, "but the battle lines have been drawn. I'm afraid it's too late."

"You're serious."

Hazard paused a moment before answering. "You've led a

sheltered life, Boston," he finally said. Tossing a towel around his neck, he continued in a moderate tone, as though discussing the merits of calling cards as a social gesture. "They're out to kill me. I consider that serious. That's why you're here. And that's why you're staying." A sudden flash of white teeth seemed to discount the undercurrent of danger. "I like my eggs soft-boiled."

He was gone in a noiseless tread, and she lay there stunned for several minutes. People didn't actually kill each other over a small section of mountain land, did they? Certainly not her father and his friends. Did they? For the first time a quiver of doubt intruded.

Wrapping the sheet around her, Blaze walked to the window and, looking out, glimpsed Hazard half screened by a clump of pines. He was swimming in a small pool contrived by damming up a portion of the rushing mountain stream. The sunlight shone off his sleek wet hair. Then he submerged, only to reappear moments later long yards away, shaking his head, droplets of water spraying like crystals from his streaming black hair.

When he started back to the cabin, all slender grace and hard rising muscle, Blaze went to the door, intending to meet him as a friendly gesture. After all, if she was truly a hostage—and it appeared the case; there was never equivocation when Hazard spoke, no matter how quiet the tone—she might as well be gracious about it. She pulled on the door latch. The door didn't respond. She tugged more determinedly. Nothing. She swore. Damn his untrusting soul. He'd locked her in!

LAST BRIDGE HOME
by
Iris Johansen

bestselling author of
THE GOLDEN BARBARIAN
and THE WIND DANCER trilogy

Jon Sandell is a man with many secrets and one remarkable power, the ability to read a woman's mind, to touch her soul, to know her every waking desire. His vital mission is to rescue a woman unaware of the danger she is in. But who will protect her from him?

She inhaled sharply as she spotted a man standing on the stone steps at the front door of the cottage. A man she had never seen before.

She pulled her car into the driveway and slowed it to a stop. The man, who was coming down the steps now, didn't look menacing, but he didn't look like the Caspar Milquetoast type either. There was something very controlled about his deliberate approach. Controlled. What an odd word to come to mind, she thought. His deeply tanned face was completely impassive, yet she had the impression he was exerting a tremendous effort to subdue forces that were seething below the surface of his calm exterior.

Standing beside her window, he bent down slightly to look at her. He spoke in a tone a level above normal so she could hear through the glass. "I'm glad you're being cautious. It's very lonely out here for a woman alone. I've been waiting for you."

He was gazing at her with an odd, almost hungry, intentness. The thought that he was only inches away, separated from her by a flimsy sheet of glass, sent a sudden shudder of fear through her. His eyes were darkly brilliant, his black brows heavy, and his bone structure was too strongly defined to ever be termed handsome. Strength. A strength so powerful it was a shock to her senses. She found herself staring at him in wide-eyed fascination.

He frowned. "For God's sake, stop looking at me like that." His voice was rough and slightly husky. "I'm not going to hurt you. I'm here to help you. I'd never—" He broke off and drew a deep breath. "Look, I'm sorry if I startled you. Let's begin again. My name is Jon Sandell and Mark Ramsey was my cousin. Perhaps he mentioned me?"

Jon Sandell. She felt a swift swell of relief and hurriedly rolled down the window. "Of course he did. I'm very glad to meet you at last." She grinned and wrinkled her nose at him. "Though you probably think I'm flighty as a loon to treat you as if you were Charles Manson. I'm not usually this uptight. I guess I have a case of prenatal jitters." She opened the door and swung her khaki-clad legs carefully to the ground. It was a massive undertaking for her to get herself out from behind the steering wheel these days. Jon Sandell stepped forward and lifted her easily from the seat and onto her feet.

"Oh, thank you, that helped a lot. I'll be with you in just a minute. I have to get the groceries out of the car. I stopped at the supermarket on the way home from school, which delayed me a bit. Have you been waiting long?"

"No." He was frowning again. "You shouldn't be out here by yourself. It may have been all right before, but now that you're—"

"—big as a house," she finished for him. She shut the car door and went around to the back of the station wagon. "This is my home. Where else would I go?" She unlocked and opened the gate. "Besides, I'm not alone. The Spauldings have a farm two miles down the road, and I have Sam."

"Sam?"

"Sam is my Heinz 57," she said with a gentle smile. "He's half Great Dane and half I-don't-know-what. Will you stay for dinner? I put a stew in the Crockpot this morning. There will be plenty for two."

He shook his head. "I can't stay but I'd like a cup of coffee and a little conversation, if it's not too much trouble."

She shook her head as she turned and headed for the steps. "Of course it's not too much trouble. I'd like to talk to you too." She glanced back over her shoulder as she unlocked the heavy

Dutch door. A smile lit her face with glowing warmth, and she said, "Mark was a stranger in these parts and not many people got to know him well enough to realize how wonderful he was. I think one of the things I missed most after he died was not being able to talk to someone who loved him as much as I did."

He was gazing at her face with the same intent expression she had noticed earlier. "I wanted to come to you then, but they wouldn't let me."

"I understood why you couldn't come to the funeral. Mark had told me you are out of the country most of the time."

"That's a fairly accurate way of phrasing it. Well, I'm here now. Why don't you go inside."

His last words were a command, spoken with the casual confidence of someone accustomed to being obeyed. Whoever "they" were, they must have been exceptionally high up in the echelon of Sandell's company to prevent him from doing anything he wanted to do. She saluted. "I'll put the coffee on, sir."

He looked up, and for the flicker of a moment there was a warm smile on his hard face. "Was I being authoritarian? I was in the military for a while and I guess you never really lose a sense of command."

"I guess you don't." She swung open the door and left it ajar for him as she moved briskly down the hall to the large kitchen which stretched the length of the rear of the cottage.

"Do you use milk or sugar?"

"No."

"Neither do I. I like my coffee black as sin and loaded with caffeine. I've been drinking it without caffeine lately because it's better for the baby, but I still miss the pick-me-up it gave me." One hand absently rubbed the hollow of her spine as she made the coffee. "And weighing as much as I do these days, it takes a heck of a lot to pick me u—" She broke off as she turned to face him. "You're looking at me very oddly. Is something wrong?"

"No. I was just thinking how beautiful you are."

She laughed with genuine amusement. "I'm not even pretty. Lord, you must have been out of the country and away from civilization and women for a long time. Where were you anyway? In the wilds of the Sahara? Remind me to introduce you to my neighbor, Serena Spaulding. She's simply gorgeous."

She took the coffee carafe and crossed the room to where he was standing. "But thanks anyway for trying to make a fat, pregnant lady feel good." She poured the steaming liquid into two cups and turned to set the carafe on the warmer. "Take off your coat and sit down." She shrugged out of her heavy navy peacoat. "I'll be right back. I have to call Sam and tell him it's chow time."

"I wouldn't think a Great Dane would have to be told."

"Usually he doesn't." Her brow knitted with a frown. "I don't know why he wasn't here to meet me. I'll be right back."

She returned in less than five minutes. "He didn't come when I called." She came slowly toward him, the worried frown still on her face. "Crazy dog. He's probably out chasing rabbits again."

Sitting down across from him at the round oak table, she straightened her shoulders as if to shrug off a burden. "Sorry, I seem to be on an anxiety kick lately. I've been blaming it on Andrew. He can't talk back yet."

"Andrew?"

"My son. It's a boy. I asked the doctor for an amniocentesis; it's a test that detects any genetic or other problems and spins off the fascinating information of the sex of the unborn child." She looked down at her coffee, her index finger gently rubbing the side of the cup. "After Mark died I needed more than a faceless entity to share my body. I needed to know my baby was all right, as well as a real person, a companion." She lifted her eyes to meet his gaze. "Do you understand?"

"Yes."

He said nothing else, yet she felt a warmth sweep through her unlike anything she had ever known. For a moment it seemed impossible to tear her gaze away from his. Her throat felt tight and she had difficulty breathing. She picked up her cup and cradled it in her palms. "I think you do. I guess it's not surprising. Mark was the most understanding man I've ever met. It must run in the family."

"I'm nothing like Mark." His tone was suddenly harsh. "Don't make the mistake of drawing comparisons that aren't there. We were as different as night and day." His lips twisted. "Inside as well as out."

What he said was true. Physically there was no resemblance between him and Mark. Jon Sandell was only a few inches taller than her five feet eight and Mark had been well over six feet. Mark also had had golden coloring with deep blue eyes and a smile as kind as summer rain. He was so incredibly handsome that people had stopped on the street to stare at him in bedazzlement. She had been dazzled herself at first and hadn't been able to believe it when he started to pursue her with gentle persistence.

There was nothing either gentle or golden about his cousin. Jon Sandell was dark and intense and composed of hard, sharp angles. She found her gaze drawn to the strong brown column of his throat and allowed it to wander down to catch the faintest glimpse of virile dark hair above the top button of his navy flannel shirt. The dark thatch of hair looked soft, springy, and suddenly, incredibly, she found her palms tingling as if she were actually touching it. The shocking sensation caused her to quickly jerk her gaze away. What had happened to her? For a moment she had felt a burst of sensuality stronger than any she had previously experienced. It was nothing, she told herself. Jon Sandell projected a raw sexuality that would have aroused a response in any woman. *I didn't mean anything.* Still, for a moment, along with the sensuality, she had felt a closeness, almost a bonding that was, in many ways, like the empathy she had known with Mark. "Well, I'm sure you're as kind as Mark or you wouldn't be making this courtesy call. I'm really grateful, Mr. Sandell."

"Jon. I've thought of you as Elizabeth for a long time." He sipped his coffee. "And I'm not kind. I'm here because I want to be." He paused. "And because I have to be."

LADY DEFIANT
by **Suzanne Robinson**
author of
LADY GALLANT and LADY HELLFIRE

Set during the tumultuous Elizabethan era in England, LADY DEFIANT tells the story of Blade, first introduced in LADY GALLANT. The disarmingly handsome Blade, now one of Queen Elizabeth's most dangerous spies, is given the task of romancing a clever young beauty named Oriel. She unknowingly holds a clue that could alter the course of history, bringing Mary, Queen of Scots to the throne of England. LADY DEFIANT is a thrilling, sensual romance from the increasingly popular Suzanne Robinson.

On sale in hardcover from Doubleday in August.
On sale in paperback from Bantam FANFARE in December.

OFFICIAL RULES TO WINNERS CLASSIC SWEEPSTAKES

No Purchase necessary. To enter the sweepstakes follow instructions found elsewhere in this offer. You can also enter the sweepstakes by hand printing your name, address, city, state and zip code on a 3" x 5" piece of paper and mailing it to: Winners Classic Sweepstakes, P.O. Box 785, Gibbstown, NJ 08027. Mail each entry separately. Sweepstakes begins 12/1/91. Entries must be received by 6/1/93. Some presentations of this sweepstakes may feature a deadline for the Early Bird prize. If the offer you receive does, then to be eligible for the Early Bird prize your entry must be received according to the Early Bird date specified. Not responsible for lost, late, damaged, misdirected, illegible or postage due mail. Mechanically reproduced entries are not eligible. All entries become property of the sponsor and will not be returned.

Prize Selection/Validations: Winners will be selected in random drawings on or about 7/30/93, by VENTURA ASSOCIATES, INC., an independent judging organization whose decisions are final. Odds of winning are determined by total number of entries received. Circulation of this sweepstakes is estimated not to exceed 200 million. Entrants need not be present to win. All prizes are guaranteed to be awarded and delivered to winners. Winners will be notified by mail and may be required to complete an affidavit of eligibility and release of liability which must be returned within 14 days of date of notification or alternate winners will be selected. Any guest of a trip winner will also be required to execute a release of liability. Any prize notification letter or any prize returned to a participating sponsor, Bantam Doubleday Dell Publishing Group, Inc., its participating divisions or subsidiaries, or VENTURA ASSOCIATES, INC. as undeliverable will be awarded to an alternate winner. Prizes are not transferable. No multiple prize winners except as may be necessary due to unavailability, in which case a prize of equal or greater value will be awarded. Prizes will be awarded approximately 90 days after the drawing. All taxes, automobile license and registration fees, if applicable, are the sole responsibility of the winners. Entry constitutes permission (except where prohibited) to use winners' names and likenesses for publicity purposes without further or other compensation.

Participation: This sweepstakes is open to residents of the United States and Canada, except for the province of Quebec. This sweepstakes is sponsored by Bantam Doubleday Dell Publishing Group, Inc. (BDD), 666 Fifth Avenue, New York, NY 10103. Versions of this sweepstakes with different graphics will be offered in conjunction with various solicitations or promotions by different subsidiaries and divisions of BDD. Employees and their families of BDD, its division, subsidiaries, advertising agencies, and VENTURA ASSOCIATES, INC., are not eligible.

Canadian residents, in order to win, must first correctly answer a time limited arithmetical skill testing question. Void in Quebec and wherever prohibited or restricted by law. Subject to all federal, state, local and provincial laws and regulations.

Prizes: The following values for prizes are determined by the manufacturers' suggested retail prices or by what these items are currently known to be selling for at the time this offer was published. Approximate retail values include handling and delivery of prizes. Estimated maximum retail value of prizes: 1 Grand Prize ($27,500 if merchandise or $25,000 Cash); 1 First Prize ($3,000); 5 Second Prizes ($400 each); 35 Third Prizes ($100 each); 1,000 Fourth Prizes ($9.00 each) ; 1 Early Bird Prize ($5,000); Total approximate maximum retail value is $50,000. Winners will have the option of selecting any prize offered at level won. Automobile winner must have a valid driver's license at the time the car is awarded. Trips are subject to space and departure availability. Certain black-out dates may apply. Travel must be completed within one year from the time the prize is awarded. Minors must be accompanied by an adult. Prizes won by minors will be awarded in the name of parent or legal guardian.

For a list of Major Prize Winners (available after 7/30/93): send a self-addressed, stamped envelope entirely separate from your entry to: Winners Classic Sweepstakes Winners, P.O. Box 825, Gibbstown, NJ 08027. Requests must be received by 6/1/93. DO NOT SEND ANY OTHER CORRESPONDENCE TO THIS P.O. BOX.

The Delaney Dynasty lives on in

The Delaney Christmas Carol

by Kay Hooper, Iris Johansen, & Fayrene Preston

Three of romantic fiction's best-loved authors present the changing face of Christmas spirit—past, present, and future—as they tell the story of three generations of Delaneys in love.

CHRISTMAS PAST by Iris Johansen

From the moment he first laid eyes on her, Kevin Delaney felt a curious attraction for the ragclad Gypsy beauty rummaging through the attic of his ranch at Killara. He didn't believe for a moment her talk of magic mirrors and second-sight, but something about Zara St. Cloud stirred his blood. Now, as Christmas draws near, a touch leads to a kiss and a gift of burning passion.

CHRISTMAS PRESENT by Fayrene Preston

Bria Delaney had been looking for Christmas ornaments in her mother's attic, when she saw him in the mirror for the first time—a stunningly handsome man with sky-blue eyes and red-gold hair. She had almost convinced herself he was only a dream when Kells Braxton arrived at Killara and led them both to a holiday wonderland of sensuous pleasure.

CHRISTMAS FUTURE by Kay Hooper

As the last of the Delaney men, Brett returned to Killara this Christmastime only to find it in the capable hands of his father's young and beautiful widow. Yet the closer he got to Cassie, the more Brett realized that the embers of their old love still burned and that all it would take was a look, a kiss, a caress, to turn their dormant passion into an inferno.